Heart of a Sinner

The Accuser

A Novel by
Shanika Roach

To submit a manuscript for our review, email us at submissions@majorkeypublishing.com

Coming Next From Major Key!

CHECK OUT THE SNEAK PEEK:
http://www.majorkeypublishing.com/sneakpeeks

Chapter 1

"Miss Murray, we agree to your terms, and a check for two hundred thousand dollars will be delivered to you by the end of the day," Dillion Charles, The CEO of Galson Energies, said to me in a polite voice, but the look in his eyes told me that he felt nothing but contempt for me.

"Thank you. Just sign these papers, and everything will be settled," My lawyer, Kimberly Lanier, said, taking the documents out of her briefcase and slid them in front of Dillion.

I was elated, and I couldn't stop the small smile that formed on my lips. I looked at Christopher Simms, the man that I was suing for sexual harassment. I could see the burning hatred in his eyes, but I didn't care. I had won and had accomplished what I set out to do.

After Dillion signed the papers, Kimberly handed another set of papers for me and Christopher to sign that stated that we couldn't talk about the incident. This is something that Dillion had demanded in negotiations. We signed the papers and then left the conference room.

Once we were outside the building, I hugged Kimberly. "Thank you again for winning another case for me."

Kimberly is a pretty brown-skinned woman with long hair that she had pulled up into a bun. "No problem at all. These men need to learn that they can't get away with saying whatever they want to say to a woman," Kimberly said with a smile.

"You're right about that," I said, but I knew it was more to it than that. But Kimberly never questioned why I needed her for these types of cases all the time.

"Call me if you shall ever need me again," Kim said, winked at me, and then got into her black Lexus ES.

I crossed the street and headed towards my silver Infiniti Q50. I was almost to my car when someone grabbed my arm from behind. I turned around to see Christopher with an incensed look on his face.

"What you did to me was cruel, and you know it," he seethed.

I looked at Christopher's handsome brown face and shrugged my shoulders. "You shouldn't have made those remarks to me and groped me the way you did," I said in a bored tone.

"Please, you flirted with me first. You said all those dirty things to me. I'm a man, of course, I was going to respond!" he yelled in my face.

"Calm down. I still didn't give you permission to touch me. You lost, and that's all there is to it. Just be thankful that you still have a job."

Christopher gave me a pitiful look and then shook his head. "You should be careful with this little game you're playing. What goes around comes around," he said and then walked away.

An eerie feeling came over me, but I quickly shook it off. I wasn't going to let him get to me. I was two hundred thousand dollars richer, and now it was time to move on to another city.

My name is Felicia Murray, and I wasn't always a cruel person. Most people consider me pretty. I have a smooth honey complexion with a small frame and curves in all the right places. I have long hair, and I stand at 5'6. I grew up in Little Rock, Arkansas. I was raised in the church. My parents Jacqueline and James Murray, were great people of God. My father was a deacon and my mother helped with different ministries in the church. I followed their example, and later took a job as the church administrator at God's Kingdom Worship Center in Little Rock when I was twenty-three years old. It was one of the largest churches in Little Rock, led by

Pastor Eugene Marks, a great man of God. I worked closely with the pastor at times, and I noticed that Pastor Eugene started giving me these looks and touching me. It was subtle touches like he would hug me a little too tight and long or rub my shoulders. I liked it, and I felt myself starting to fall for him. He was thirty-eight years old and very handsome, but he was also very married and had two kids. I tried to fight the temptation, but we started having an affair. It was hard keeping it from everyone. He told me he loved me and even said he was thinking about leaving his wife, Nadine. That was music to my ears, but I didn't know how he would do that being a Pastor and all. We had an affair for two years without being discovered until I attended an out of town conference with him. A reporter saw me exiting his hotel and reported the story. It was a huge story, and it was obvious what was going on since I wasn't supposed to be at the conference in the first place. Word spread, and after further investigation, it didn't take long for the public to discover we had been having an affair for two years.

I was embarrassed and ashamed, and so was my family. But it was also a sign of relief for me because now Eugene could leave his wife since everyone already knew. He quickly crushed my dreams when he told me that it was a mistake for him to get involved with me, that he loved his wife and wasn't leaving her. I watched as he gave television interviews stating how sorry he was with his wife by his side. The public eventually forgave him but was not so forgiving of me. I was relieved of my duties as church administrator because his wife didn't want me working that position anymore. I couldn't get a job anywhere else. People who weren't even in church didn't want me working for them. People at the church shunned me and even my own family. My mom and dad gave me a lecture about adultery. I left the church, but staying in Little Rock was hard because I didn't have the support of anyone except my cousin Latrice. Her mother and father moved to New York City when she turned twenty, so she didn't see them often, and we grew even closer. She didn't condone what I had done, but she said that everyone deserved forgiveness. But people didn't see it that way. I was a pretty young woman who almost brought down a great man of God. They wouldn't forgive me, but they forgave him, and that hurt me deeply. I called Eugene and asked him to meet up with me. He reluctantly snuck away to see me, and I told him how much I loved him and asked how he could do this to me. He told me he was sorry and that he never meant to hurt me. His words soothed my aching heart, and that led to us having sex. After that, I had some hope that maybe he changed his mind. But all my calls went unanswered after that, and I knew I had to leave Little Rock.

I left Little Rock and moved to Oklahoma. Shortly after moving there, I discovered I was pregnant as a result of my last night of passion with Eugene. I thought about calling him and telling him, but I knew that me being pregnant wouldn't make a difference. When people found out that I was carrying his baby, it would make things worse for me, so I had an abortion.

I later regretted the decision because I knew I wasn't thinking clearly. I was mad and broken-hearted, but what was done was done, and I went into a deep depression, but then my sadness turned to rage, and I wanted payback. Powerful men like Eugene could do whatever they wanted to do and not suffer any major consequences, but a woman's life would forever be blemished. At that moment, I decided I would target men in positions of power and bring them down.

I started my plan in Oklahoma, I took a job at a large company as an administrative assistant, and I would flirt with one of the bosses. When they flirted back and started making inappropriate comments, I would file a sexual harassment lawsuit. In fear of their position and reputation, and not wanting their wives or significant others to find out, they would settle quietly. It was all fun and games to me, and it felt good to pay men back for their weaknesses. I didn't have to be a victim if I didn't want to. I would then move to another state or town and do the same thing over again. I had done this five times in the last five years. My bank account was looking pretty good from the settlements. I could get away with it because the companies I worked for kept the incidents quiet and couldn't talk about it if another job called asking about a reference. I was now thirty years old. My last stop was Oregon, where I made Christopher pay.

My next stop was Las Vegas. I felt even bigger things would be in store for me there.

Chapter 2

I arrived in Las Vegas two weeks later and was enjoying the beautiful city. I had bought a nice condo and already put in a job resume at Dutton and Harrell law firm. It was run by attorneys Carlos Dutton and Earl Harrell, and it was one of the largest law firms in Las Vegas. Dutton and Harrell had many high-profile clients, including celebrities, and I was looking forward to working there. I was looking at a picture of Carlos Dutton I had pulled up on my laptop. He was a very handsome man with wavy hair and a nice bronze complexion. He looked like he was mixed with maybe Mexican. I was going to set my sights on him. He is thirty-eight and has a wife and child. He would be the perfect target, and I would really enjoy flirting with him.

I ordered Chinese takeout, and it was delivered twenty minutes later. I was just about to eat my kung pao chicken when my cell phone rang. It was my cousin Latrice.

I answered the call. "Hey. How's everything in Las Vegas?" Patrice asked.

"It's going great, and I'm settling in nicely. I put in a job resume at Dutton and Harrell, and I should be hearing back from them soon."

Latrice paused for a second, and I already knew what she was thinking. "I hope you're not going to be up to your old tricks again."

I sighed. "I only throw the bait out there. It's up to them if they take it or not."

"I don't like the way you're playing with these men's lives. You should really get back in church."

Get back into church? Was she kidding? That's where all of my problems started and what led me to the worst pain I felt in my life. Eugene was a leader, and he sexually harassed me. If only I had recognized it then instead of falling for his charm. "No thanks, I'll pass on that," I said sarcastically.

"I'm not trying to judge you. I'm just worried about you, that's all."

Her words caused my annoyance to come down some. "I know you are, but there's no need to be. In fact, why don't you come and visit me," I suggested.

"I don't know if I can right now. With work and the new baby and all."

Latrice is a physician's assistant and married with a four-month-old daughter. "You should still find the time to come and bring baby Casey with you."

"I'll see if I can, but you should come and visit me sometimes."

I became stiff at her suggestion. I was not going to step foot back in Little Rock, and she knew why. "You should hang out in Vegas with me."

Latrice laughed, and she knew I was avoiding her suggestion about coming to Little Rock. "Maybe I will. Take care of yourself and I love you."

"I love you too," I said, and we ended the call. I really missed my cousin. We were the same age and had always been close. I knew it would be much easier for me to visit her in Little Rock, but I refused to go there.

I sat back and enjoyed my food, thinking about my new job prospect. It took about a week, but Dutton and Harrell finally called me about an interview. I was delighted to know that Carlos Dutton was interviewing me for the position since I would be working for him.

I put on a nice skirt and blouse. The skirt outlined my figure without being too provocative, and the blouse only showed a hint of cleavage. I didn't want to be too overt. I would work on that once I got the job.

I was a bundle of nerves as I pulled into the parking lot of the law firm, but I had to remind myself that I had gone to plenty of interviews, and I knew just what to say. I exited my car and walked up to the building.

I went inside and told the receptionist that I was there for an interview. She picked up the phone and told the person she was talking to my name and that I was there for an interview. She hung up the phone then told me to go to the second floor to wait and that Carlos Dutton would be with me shortly. I took the elevator to the second floor and took a seat in the lobby area. The receptionist on that floor smiled at me and told me that Carlos would be with me in a moment. I looked around and was impressed by what I saw. It was a nice huge law firm. About twenty minutes later, the receptionist told me that he was ready to see me now. She told me that his office was right around the corner.

I thanked her and then walked around the corner to the door with his name written in gold letters. I took a deep breath then knocked on the door.

"Come in," he said.

I opened the door and walked inside his office. Carlos gave me a huge smile and stood up. He looked dapper in his expensive suit. His pictures didn't do him justice because he was even better looking in person.

"Hello, Miss Murray. Are you ready for your interview?" He said and extended his hand for me to shake.

I shook his hand, surprised at his friendliness. "Yes, I'm ready," I said. He sat down, and I sat down in the chair across from him. I observed his office. His office was decorated nicely and he had his diplomas and awards on the wall. He had achieved a lot.

"I went over your resume, and you have a lot of administrative experience. But in the legal field, it's a different playing field, and sometimes the workload can be strenuous. Do you think that you can handle that?"

"Yes, I can handle it."

He smiled at me. "That's what I like to hear. You can start on Monday."

"Monday?" I said, surprised.

"Yes, is that too soon?"

"No, not at all. I just didn't know I would be starting so soon. But I'm happy about that," I said and smiled at him.

"Great, I have a meeting to get to, but if you can come back in a couple of hours, I will show you around the office, then fill you in on exactly what I will be having you do."

"Sure, I can be back then."

"Good. Welcome to Dutton and Harrell."

"Thank you," I said as I stared at this gorgeous man before me knowing I was going to send him on a roller coaster ride that he wouldn't see coming.

I left the office, got something to eat, and then arrived back just in time for him to show me around the office. He introduced me to his staff and then explained my job to me. After he showed me around, he asked if I wanted to go to lunch with him. I agreed, even though I was still kind of full from my lunch earlier.

He took me to a nice quiet café around the corner from the law firm. We talked about general things, and he was so pleasant and charming. I liked him right away. Here he was being so nice to me, and I was planning something that could potentially destroy his life or career, but I couldn't worry about that. He deserved to pay just like all the others.

Chapter 3

It's two weeks later, and things had been going well at Dutton and Harrell. I had been getting the hang of things, and it was a very busy environment. I didn't get that many chances to be alone with Carlos because he was always so busy with cases, and I stayed busy typing up his reports. The short times that I did get to, I tried to feel him out a little, but it was hard to get anything out of him because he was so distracted by his work. When I did have his attention, he could be hot and cold at times. Sometimes he was very nice to me, and the next, he was yelling out demands. I tried not to take it personally because I knew how much stress lawyers could be under. He was also in meetings with his private investigator Dexter.

I was at my desk and finally finished typing up a ten-page document for Carlos. I got up from my desk and knocked on his office door. He told me to come in. He had a bunch of papers in front of him, and he had a tired look on his face.

"Sorry to interrupt, I wanted to give you the documents that I finished typing up."

"Oh yes," he said, perking up. "I needed those to give to Mr. Daily in the morning. You're so great, I don't know what I would do without you," he said and smiled at me.

That was my opening. "That's why I'm here," I said, walked over to his desk and handed him the documents. He put them in a leather folder and put the folder in his desk drawer.

"You look like you need to relax. Let me give you a massage," I said and walked behind his desk.

"No, I don't think you should do that," he started to object, but I silenced him by beginning to massage his shoulders. "Wow, that feels good," he said and moaned.

I smiled because I had him exactly where I wanted him. I massaged his shoulders for a few seconds more than I bent down and whispered in his ear. "Just think of what else I can do that can feel good." My words caused his body to stiffen, and I was afraid that I had pushed too hard.

"Yes, what you're doing feels nice, but we shouldn't be doing this," he said.

I slowly removed my hands from his shoulder and walked around the other side of the desk. "I'm sorry, I just saw you were tense, and I wanted to help."

"That's okay, but if you would excuse me, I have to get back to work," he said in a sharp tone.

"Sure thing," I said, a little surprised at how quickly his mood changed. There was nothing else for me to say, so I left his office. The way his mood switched was strange, but I knew I moved too quickly. I could kick myself for pushing too hard. Now he was going to be extra careful around me.

I was disappointed, but I shook it off and finished my work for the rest of the day. The next few days, Carlos kept his guard up around me and only talked to me about the work he needed me to do. His wife, who was a beautiful Asian woman named Mindy, came by the office to take him to lunch. She was very sweet and polite to me, if she only knew. I would just tread lightly until another opportunity arose.

The rest of the week went by. It was Friday evening, and I had just returned home from work. I was excited because my cousin Latrice was coming to visit me tomorrow. She was bringing Casey, and I was glad to be meeting my niece in person. I took a shower and changed into a pair of fitted red jeans and a cream-colored blouse, and I put on a pair of stiletto heels. I fixed my hair and makeup, grabbed my brown leather Gucci purse and drove to the mall.

When I arrived at the mall, I began looking in stores. I was going to do some shopping for myself, Latrice, and Casey. I bought a few pairs of designer jeans and purses for Latrice and me. I knew Latrice wouldn't want me spending so much money on her, but she deserved it. I was glad that she took the time to fly out here to see me. I offered to pay for her plane ticket, but she wouldn't hear of it.

Next, I went to the baby boutique and start browsing all the beautiful baby clothes. I started to feel sad as I looked at the baby clothes because I thought about the baby I aborted, but I quickly shoved those feelings deep down inside. I bought a lot of baby clothes for Casey, including a bassinet and stroller, so much stuff that one of the staff members offered to help me carry the bags to my car. I was grateful for that.

After leaving the mall, I drove home and had to make a couple of trips to get all the clothes inside. Once I got all the bags inside, I took the baby and the things I brought for Latrice in one of the guestrooms. After doing that, I plopped down on the couch, took off my heels, and propped my feet on the coffee table. I was tired and needed to rest for a minute.

After resting for about ten minutes, I went to the guestroom, put the bassinet together, and then I ordered some take out and watched television. I was relaxed and ready for my cousin's visit the next day.

Chapter 4

The next morning, I was super excited as I drove to the airport to pick up Latrice. I was realizing how much I missed her. I hadn't made any friends since I had been away from Little Rock. When I arrived at the airport, it didn't take me long to spot out Latrice standing holding Casey in her arms. Next to her was a car seat and a large bag. She looked great. Latrice is light brown with a small frame, but I noticed she had curves now since giving birth. She filled out the knee length, short sleeve blue dress she wore nicely.

As I walked closer to her, she spotted me, and her face broke out in a huge smile. When I reached her, I gave her a huge side hug, being careful not to squeeze the baby, and looked at baby Casey. She was a gorgeous baby with a head full of hair, and she looked a lot like Casey. "You don't know how happy I am to see you. You look great, and Casey is beautiful," I said as softly touched her cheek. She was sound asleep.

"Thanks and look at you. I see you've been taking great care of yourself," she said.

"I try," I said. "Come on, my car is right this way." I picked up her bag and car seat.

We walked through the airport to my car. "Wow, this is a nice car," Latrice said as she carefully put Casey in the car seat and strapped her in the backseat.

"Thank you, I've had it for about a year now," I said, putting her bag in the trunk. We got into my car, and I drove away from the airport onto the highway.

"I'm loving this city already. I never thought I would be in Las Vegas," Latrice said as she looked out the window.

"Yes, it's a nice city. Maybe I could show you around."

"That will be nice," Latrice said.

When we arrived at the condo, Latrice was in awe of my place. "This is so nice," she said as she admired my furniture.

I smiled. "Thank you. Come follow me. I have some things to show you." I walked towards the guest room with Latrice following behind me, carrying Casey in her arms.

"You bought all this, and you even bought a bassinet and stroller?" She said in amazement as she looked at the numerous bags on the bed and floor. She walked over to the bassinet and put Casey inside. She was still asleep. I was a little surprised she was sleeping through all this.

"Yes, things for Casey and a few things for you as well."

"I appreciate all this, but you really didn't have to buy me anything."

"Of course, I did," I said.

Latrice looked through all the bags, and she was pleased with all the purchases. "You're great," she said.

"Come on, I'll order us some food. You must be hungry," I said.

"Yes, I'm hungry, but I'll cook something instead."

"No, you just got here. You should just relax and eat take-out."

"I'm fine, and I bet you eat takeout all the time," Latrice said with a laugh and left the room. I followed behind her as she walked into my kitchen and begin looking through the cabinets. Then she looked in the fridge, and she pulled out a pack of chicken and a bag of mixed vegetables.

"I'll make some garlic pepper chicken, and we can eat some stir-fried vegetables to go with it," Latrice suggested.

"That sounds good." I didn't cook much at all, and it was

going to be nice to have a home-cooked meal. "I'll help you," I said, pulled out the cutting board, got the vegetables out of the fridge, and began cutting them up.

Latrice began cutting up the chicken. "I cook but not as often as I would like because I work long hours. I used some of my vacation time so I could come here and visit you."

"I know you must had a time convincing Steven to let you come here."

Latrice gave me a small smile. "Don't worry about Steven; he'll come around."

Steven was Latrice's husband and he didn't care for me at all. Latrice was worried about the lifestyle I was living, and she voiced these concerns to her husband. Big mistake, because he didn't want Latrice to have a relationship with me. He felt that I could be a bad influence on her. Steven has an executive position at a large corporation, and he knows what kind of damage a sexual harassment lawsuit can do to a man's career. So the fact that I was purposely trying to bait men into doing it was unspeakable to him. Latrice kept her relationship with me anyway, and I was grateful that she stuck by me when no one else would.

We finished making dinner and ate. During dinner, Latrice told me how much she liked her job and how she really enjoyed taking care of patients. Latrice was such a compassionate person that genuinely cared about people, so she picked a perfect career.

When we finished eating, Latrice went to check on Casey and discovered she was awake, ready to be fed. I asked her if I could feed Casey, and she said it would be fine.

Latrice made a bottle of milk for Casey, and then she handed me the bottle. I was seated on the couch and Latrice sat next to me. I held Casey in my arms and loved the way she felt in my arms. I fed her and watched her lovingly while she drank the milk. She was so beautiful, and as she sucked the bottle, I started thinking of the child I aborted, the child that I would never get to hold in my arms. I was overcome with a feeling of sadness. I tried to stuff the feelings inside like I usually do, but my feelings disobeyed me, and tears began to spill down my cheeks.

"What's wrong?" Casey asked, gently rubbing my back.

I couldn't speak. I started crying uncontrollably, and Latrice took her daughter out of my arms. Latrice moved to the couch across from me and fed her daughter. She gave me worried glances as she fed Casey. After she fed her, she burped her and took her in the guest room. Latrice returned about twenty minutes later and sat next to me.

"Now, please tell me what's wrong."

By now, my sobbing had quieted. "It's nothing. I'm fine, really."

"No, you are not fine. Tell me what's wrong; maybe I can help."

I looked at the concerned look on Latrice's face, and I was tired of carrying this pain around with me. I hadn't told anyone about this. Maybe now was the best time to release this.

"When I left Little Rock, I found out I was pregnant, but I was so hurt and angry with Eugene because I knew he wasn't going to be there for me. I just..." I stopped talking, not wanting to say the next words.

"You what? Go ahead and say it," Latrice said anxiously.

"I had an abortion," I said, and I felt a huge weight leave my shoulders.

Latrice stared at me for a moment. "I wish you would have told me that you were pregnant. I would have helped you. You didn't have to deal with it alone."

"I know you would have helped me, but at the time, I didn't think having Eugene's baby would have been the best thing for me, but shortly after I did it, I realized it was the biggest mistake of my life."

"Now it all makes sense," Latrice said with a thoughtful look on her face.

"What makes sense?"

"Why you began to be so cold towards men and wanted to set them up? You haven't dealt with the feelings about your abortion, and until you do, you're going to keep doing these cruel things," Latrice sighed. "The heart of a sinner. Until you deal with all this pain, you will continue to do this."

Her words convicted me, but I was too stubborn to admit it to her. "Maybe it's cruel, but they don't have to go for it."

Latrice shook her head. "I bet you are already working on your next victim."

My silence was confirmation.

"I really wish you would stop doing this. You're a beautiful young woman who has so much going for yourself. You can't let what Eugene did to you destroy your life."

"It's not destroying my life. I have a lot of money to buy nice things with all the settlement money that I racked up over the years."

"I know, but sooner or later, it will catch up to you. God has a grace period, and He's being patient because He knows your pain, but you can't keep doing this to people at not expect any consequences."

Her words gave me the same eerie feeling that I got when Christopher repeated similar words to me. To be honest, I never really worried about the consequences of what I was doing because I was focused on the wrong that was done to me. And the fact that it caused me to make a decision that still haunted me to this day. I could feel my spirit trying to tell me to listen, but I just couldn't give in to it. I had been doing this for so long that I was so used to it being my comfort. I was afraid to turn it all over to God because the pain of it all was too much. No, it was better that I just cover my feelings with what I was doing. It had been working for me this long.

I dried my tears with the back of my hand. "I appreciate your concern, but how I live my life is my business, and I'm happy about my decisions."

"Okay, but you, breaking down just now, just proved that you're not as happy as you think. I will continue to pray for you, though."

It was tense and awkward after that, but we managed to get through the rest of the day. The next day we all went to Centennial Hills Park. It was a nice park in Las Vegas that had a lot of activities, so we had fun. Latrice and I talked as she strolled Casey around the park. We didn't mention anything about our conversation yesterday. I was glad that we were back on a better note.

Chapter 5

It was Monday morning, and I was on my way to work. The weekend was over, and I was glad because it was time for me to refocus. It was great spending time with Latrice and Casey, but it was very emotional for me, and I didn't like feeling emotional and out of control.

When I arrived at work, I went inside the building and quickly took the elevator to the second floor to start my day. I quickly learned that it was going to be a very busy day. The firm was hired by actor Alton Brewer, a twenty-seven-year old dark-haired Caucasian man. He was arrested Saturday night for raping and beating twenty-three-year-old, Julia Neil. She was found last night by one of her neighbors in her apartment building. The neighbor got suspicious when she found her apartment door slightly ajar. She found Julia barely conscious, but she managed to say Alton's name. The neighbor told the paramedics and the police that she said the name Alton before losing consciousness.

The police looked at the surveillance tape and saw that Alton was the last person that visited her before her rape and beating. Things weren't looking good for Alton because his DNA was found inside of Julia's body, but he admitted that he had consensual sex with Julia that night after meeting her at a night club. He insisted that someone must have come and beat her after he left her apartment. It was a challenging case, and Alton has even more problems because he has a girlfriend of three years, and I could only imagine how she is feeling right now.

I was busy most of the day typing up report after report, but I managed to finally take a break, and I knocked on Carlos' office door.

"Come in," he said.

I walked in his office and saw that he was busy looking at some papers on his desk. "I finished typing up that last report. I was going to get something to eat, and I wanted to know if you wanted anything. That's unless if you are planning to have lunch with your wife today," I threw out there to see if she would be coming in. I wanted to know if she was going to be popping up.

I was surprised to see an irritated look come across Carlos' face. "No, she's definitely not bringing me any lunch," he said in a terse voice.

So, there was trouble in paradise. I saw this as another opportunity. "Is everything all right?" I asked him.

"I don't want to burden you with my problems, but I would really appreciate it if you would pick me something up to eat. I've been busy all day and didn't realize I was hungry until now."

"Sure thing, what would like to eat."

"Surprise me," he said and winked at me. He reached in his wallet and handed me two twenty-dollar bills. That should be enough to cover our lunch.

"I will, and yes, this should be enough," I said. I left the building and drove to Jesse's Subs. They had great subs. I order us two turkey and cheese subs and two lemonades. I felt like I couldn't go wrong with that choice. I paid for the food and drove back to the office. Once inside I went to the second floor and to Carlos' office.

I tried to give Carlos his change, but he told me to keep it. We sat at the table in the corner of the office and began to eat our food. I could see Carlos beginning to relax.

"This case is so huge, and I really don't need any distractions. My wife's been complaining about the hours I'm working, and she was really upset about me missing my son's soccer game today. But what can I do? I have to make a living. She has a hobby that she makes money off, but I bring in the big bucks. That's why we're able to afford the huge house we live in and all those fancy clothes that she likes to wear, but she never complains about the money," Carlos said, exasperated.

I didn't expect for him to open up to me that much, but I'm pleased that he did. "I understand your point. Sacrifices have to be made. If I had a smart, handsome guy like you, I wouldn't be complaining."

"Oh yeah," Carlos said slyly, and then his eyes traveled to my cleavage. I had been making sure that I exposed a healthy portion of it now.

"Yes indeed," I said and winked at him.

"You know I'm very attracted to you, but I have been trying to be professional."

"You should do what you feel," I said, egging him on.

"Maybe I will," he said and continued to eat his food.

We finished up our meal with him telling me all the notes he needed me to type up. He changed the subject on me and was back to being professional, but I knew it wouldn't be long until he made his move on me.

After our meal, I finished up my work for the day, and then went home. Once home, I changed into lounging clothes and ordered some takeout. As I was waiting, my cell phone rang. I answered the call and was surprised to hear my mother's voice.

"Hey, Felicia," my mother said in a soft voice.

"Hi, Mom," I said, shocked that she had called me. My relationship with her had been strained since I left Little Rock. I only called her on her birthday and Mother's Day, and my relationship with my father was pretty much the same. I couldn't get over how they didn't stick by me and continued to serve under Eugene after what he did to me.

"I know you're surprised to hear from me, but I wanted to check on you because I was worried about you."

That made me suspicious. Why was she all of a sudden worried about me? "Why are you worried about me?"

"Well, I talked to Latrice, and she told me you were very upset, so I wanted to know if you're all right."

Just as I suspected, Latrice had said something to my mother. I was so upset. How could she say something to my mother about me? My parents had no idea what I had been doing since I left Little Rock.

"What did she say to you?" I asked curtly.

"Calm down, honey. She just told me that you broke down because of all the pain you been carrying around."

"Save it, Mom. You haven't been worried about my pain all the years I've been gone. You've been too busy sucking up to that hypocrite, Eugene Marks."

"Now you just hold on a minute. I'm still your mother, and you watch how you talk to me. You want to blame everything on Eugene, but you are the one who chose to get into bed with a married man, so you can't put everything on him."

My mother's words wounded me. I couldn't believe she was talking to me this way. "You know what, you don't really care about what's going on with me. You're just calling because Latrice probably asked you to. I don't need your fake sympathy, Mom!" I yelled and slammed down the phone.

I know she was my mother, and I probably shouldn't have hung up on her the way I did, but she should have been more caring and concerned, instead of throwing my mistakes in my face. Tears were threatening to spill down my cheeks, but I refuse to let the fall. And Latrice. I couldn't believe her. She told my mother what I revealed to her in confidence. It took a lot for me to tell her that, and she just blurts it out to my mother just like that. If I wanted my mother to know, I would have told her.

I picked up my cell phone, but my hands were trembling. I was so angry. I calmed myself down and then hit her number in my contacts, but my call went to voicemail.

"Latrice, call me when you get this. It's very important," I said and then hung up the phone. She was off work this week, so I expected for her to call me back soon.

When my food arrived fifteen minutes later, I couldn't eat because I had lost my appetite. I blindly watched tv for the next hour until Latrice finally called me back.

"Hey, Felicia. What's going on?"

"Like you don't know. How dare you tell my mother the things I told you."

"Wait a minute, calm down. I didn't tell her about your abortion. I just told her she needed to call and check on you because you were hurting worse than we all realized," she explained.

"You shouldn't have told her that. She called me acting all concerned then threw in my face my mistake with Eugene."

"I'm sorry. You guys need to really talk and try to be calm without throwing blame at each other."

"I don't know if I can."

"You should try. She's your mother, and she loves you."

"She loves me, but you had to tell her to call me and check up on me."

"To be fair, you don't call her that much either."

"That's because she turned her back on me but continued to serve that devil in disguise Eugene."

"She was just disappointed in you. We all were, and Eugene isn't that bad."

"So, you're taking his side too?" I asked, feeling my anger growing.

"No, I'm not taking his side. I'm just saying everyone deserves a second chance."

"Listen, I'm going to go now." I was sick of hearing all this, and I certainly didn't want to start thinking about Eugene. If I was totally honest with myself, a small part of myself still loved him.

"Okay, and I'm sorry that I talked to your mother. I promise I won't do that again."

"It's okay. I'll talk to you later," I said and hung up the phone.

I went upstairs and ran water in my Jacuzzi tub. While I soaked in the tub, I thought about everything. I had made some progress at work today with my plan, but only to have it ruined by my mother's call. That called stirred up emotions in me again. I didn't want to feel any of that. I turned my thoughts to the next day, and I knew I was a step closer to trapping Carlos.

Chapter 6

The next morning, I dressed in a shorter skirt with a split on each side, and a tight blouse that showed more cleavage than usual. I sprayed on some perfume and did my hair and make-up. I was determined to trap Carlos today. The conversation with my mother last night, and the emotions that it stirred up only fueled my determination.

After I was dressed, I looked myself over in my full-length mirror and was satisfied with what I saw. I ate a quick bowl of cereal and then drove to work. When I arrived at work, I strutted through the doors with a purpose. I spoke to a few of the employees as I walked to the elevator and took it to the second floor. I walked down the hallway and to my desk. I put my things down and turned on the computer. I was about to start working when Carlos stepped out of his office.

"Can I see you in my office?" he asked me.

"Sure," I said, stood up, and walked into his office.

He closed the door behind us, walked over to me, and softly stroked my cheek. "You know I was thinking about all the things you've been saying to me, and I'm ready to take you up on your offer," he said, grabbing my face and kissing me.

I was so shocked by his sudden move that I let it happen. I stopped him when he tried to force his tongue down my throat. His breath tasted like alcohol, and I couldn't believe he had been drinking.

I pulled away from him. "Please don't do that again," I said, not feeling his actions. Something seemed really off about him.

"Why not? You've been basically throwing yourself at me, and now that I want to collect, you're backing out on me?" He said with a glazed look in his eyes. Then he grabbed my wrist tightly and then forcefully backed me into the wall, causing me to bang my back hard.

"Stop it. I never asked for this," I pleaded, feeling scared.

"Come on, you know you want it," he said and started kissing me roughly. Then he tried to put his hands up my skirt.

I wanted him to make a move on me, but I never expected it to go like this. He was acting like he had lost his mind or something. I managed to move my mouth away from him. "Stop!" I yelled loudly.

An irate look flashed in his eyes. "Stop yelling," he said and jerked my head back so hard that my head bumped against the wall, dazing me for a minute.

He had my underwear down to my knees when Lucille walked in. She was the receptionist on our floor. "Oh God! What's going on in here?"

Carlos turned around and looked at her. "Lucille, it's not what you think," he tried to explain. It was like he was finally coming to his senses and just now realizing what he had done.

Lucille ignored him and walked over to me. "Are you okay?" she asked with a worried look on her face.

I pulled my underwear up and fixed my skirt. "I think so," I said, holding my head. I was feeling dizzy from the blow.

"Come with me. We're going to talk to Mr. Harrell," she said and helped guide me out of the room. She rolled her eyes at Carlos as we walked out of the office.

We walked around the corner to Mr. Harrell's office. A few of the other employees were looking at me with a confused look on her face. His administrative assistant tried to stop us when we were about to knock on his door.

"You can't go in there right now; he's meeting with the assistant district attorney about Alton's Brewer's case," she said.

"This can't wait," Lucille insisted.

His assistant looked at me holding my head and the dishevelment of my clothes, and she picked up the phone to tell Mr. Harrell that it was an emergency. We sat on the leather chairs in the lobby area, and five minutes later, the ADA left, and Mr. Harrell motioned for us to come into his office. We walked into his office, and Lucille closed the door behind us.

"This better be good."

"It is. I caught Mr. Dutton assaulting Felicia."

"What?" he asked with an astonished look on his face. He looked at me and took in my appearance. "Lucille, let me talk to Felicia alone. I'll bring you back in for a moment to get your side of it."

"Okay," Lucille said. She gave me a sympathetic look before leaving the office.

"Please have a seat, Felicia," he said. I sat in the chair across from him.

"Now, what happened?"

"Mr. Dutton called me into his office. He kissed me, and when I tried to stop him, he roughly grabbed my wrist, forced me against the wall, and I bumped my head hard. He then proceeded to grope me and tried to remove my underwear."

"I'm sorry that happened to you, but do you know where his actions came from?"

"What are you implying?" I asked, already knowing where he was getting at.

Before he could respond, Carlos rushed into his office. "Don't listen to a word she's saying, Earl. She's been practically waving her panties in my face, and when I make a move, she acts like I did something wrong!" he yelled.

Mr. Harrell stood up. "Lower your voice. I can tell you have been drinking. You need to leave this office for today. I'll talk to you tomorrow about everything and what steps we need to take."

"Steps? What steps?" he asked angrily.

"You were caught assaulting your assistant. She can press charges, so you need to go home and pull yourself together. Obviously, you haven't been taking care of yourself the way you should," Mr. Harrell said.

I was curious about exactly what he meant by Carlos not taking care of himself the way he should. I could feel Carlos' eyes on me, but I refused to look at him. I heard the office door close, so I knew he left.

"Listen, I'm sorry this happened to you, but I need to know if you did anything to encourage his behavior?"

"That shouldn't matter. I'm thinking about pressing charges against him because he left bruises on my wrists. Look at the purple bruises on my wrists, and I still feel kind of dizzy," I said, holding my arms out so he could see my bruises.

A concerned look flashed across Mr. Harrell's face as he looked at my bruises. "I'm sorry, we need to get you to the hospital immediately. I'll get the driver to take you to the hospital, but I trust that you will be discreet about this."

"You mean not tell the doctors what really happened to me?"

"Just until we can figure things out. Carlos is a good man; he can just get wound up at times."

I frowned. *What was he trying to tell me about him*? "Is there something about Carlos I should know?"

"I'll get the driver to take you to the hospital now, and I'll tell Lucille to bring your things," he said, avoiding the subject. He picked up the phone and called Lucille to tell her to bring my things and for the driver to pull around to the front of the building.

Lucille came to the office a few minutes later and handed me my purse. "I'll walk you out," she said.

"I'll be in touch with you, Felicia," Mr. Harrell said before I left the office.

Lucille walked with me out of the building, and we ignored the curious looks everyone was giving us.

"I tell you men with a little power think they can do anything to a woman," Lucille said when we exited the building.

"Thanks, Lucille," I said.

"Don't mention it. Now, I know Harrell was trying to tell you to keep quiet but don't let them bully you into being silent."

"I'll keep that in mind," I said and then got into the back seat of the company limousine.

As the driver drove me to the hospital, I couldn't help but think about how things didn't go according to plan. Usually, at this point, I would be happy that the man fell for my trap, but now I was scared because I felt I had bit off more than I could chew.

Chapter 7

When I arrived at the emergency room, they took me to a room, where I told the doctor that I was feeling dizzy after tripping on the stairs and hitting my head. She examined my head and located a small bump. The doctor had me change into a gown and noticed the bruises on my wrist. She asked me what happened, but I refused to explain any further. She told me that there were people I could talk to if I was in an abusive relationship, and I assured her that I wasn't. I could tell she didn't believe me, but she took me to an exam room where I had a head CT.

It was later confirmed that I had a slight concussion. The doctor told me that I had to stay overnight for observation unless I had someone that I lived with that could watch over me. I told her that I didn't, so I had to stay. I was really upset and didn't want to spend the night in the hospital, but I had no choice. I had a headache, and I was still in a little shock about the way things went down. I was physically assaulted by Carlos, and now I had to spend the night in the hospital.

I called Kimberly and told her what happened. She was in shock that things went that far, and she told me that she would fly to Vegas in the morning to put together an offer for Carlos. She said that she could get me a lump sum of money from him in exchange for me not pressing charges. She told me to make sure I left with all the paperwork from my hospital visit. Instead of feeling excited about another payday, I was feeling nervous. Something was off about Carlos, and I asked Kimberly could she look in his background and she said she would get right on it. I texted her my address, and she told me she would call me in the morning when she landed in Vegas.

After talking to Kimberly, I settled back in bed. I watched television with the nurses interrupting me throughout the night to make sure I was okay. When morning came, the doctor examined me and determined that I could go home. I told her that I would need a copy of all the paperwork from my hospital say. She wrote me a prescription for Ibuprofen and determined that I could go home. Before I left, she tried to talk to me again about what really happened, but I stuck to my story.

The doctor gave me all the paperwork and told me that I should rest for the next few days. I was finally discharged from the hospital, and I called a taxi to pick me up. The taxi arrived fifteen minutes later, and I told him to take me to Dutton and Harrell because I needed to get my car. Once there, I paid him and hurried to my car not wanting anyone to see me. I got into my car and drove to the pharmacy nearby to get my prescription filled. I was glad it took them only ten minutes to fill it, and I was happy to be on my way home.

When I arrived home, I immediately took a shower. Afterward, I put on jeans and a blouse and went to the kitchen to eat a light breakfast of toast and scrambled eggs. I drank a glass of orange juice with it and took an ibuprofen.

I was almost finished with my meal when my cell phone rung. I looked down at the number and saw that it was Dutton and Harrell calling. I sighed and answered the phone.

"Hello, Felicia. How are you feeling this morning?" Harrell asked me.

"I'm feeling okay. I was diagnosed with a concussion and have a headache still."

"Oh my, I'm sorry to hear that," he paused for a minute before speaking. "Do you feel up to coming in today because I want to talk to you along with Carlos to discuss the incident yesterday?"

"Actually, I'm meeting with my lawyer this morning, and we may be in to talk to you later today."

"A lawyer? I see. What is it that you want, Miss Murray?" he asked in a tense voice.

"I'll tell you all that once I have talked things over with my lawyer. I have to go now. I'm eating breakfast."

"Okay, I'll talk to you later on," he said, and we ended the call.

I finished my breakfast, went into the living room, and turned on the tv, and my eyes went wide when the news reporter began to talk.

"We just received word today that Carlos Dutton, from the law firm Dutton and Harrell, was said to have assaulted his assistant. His assistant's name isn't being released. As you know, Dutton and Harrell is representing Alton Brewer in the rape case of Julia Neil. Dutton and Harrell have represented and won many high-profile cases, but I don't know how things are going to work out now that this rumor is going around. Just to be clear, Carlos Dutton hasn't been charged with anything. We will keep you informed when more details are being made available."

My heart started racing, and knots began to form in my stomach. I wanted this to be kept quiet. There was no way that I wanted my name to be out there for the world to know. I already went through that before. This was supposed to happen quietly. Someone inside the office must have talked to the press. I hope they didn't get my name. My already aching head began to throb. I laid back on the couch, and before I knew it, I fell asleep.

I woke up when my cell phone rang. It was Kimberly.

"Hey, I'm in Vegas, and I'm leaving the rental car place now. I should be at your condo in about five minutes," she said.

"Okay, I'll see you then," I said, and we ended the call.

I went to the bathroom to get myself together, washing my face. I was feeling tired and my stomach was still in knots. It was probably from the stress of everything. I left the bathroom and went into the living room to wait for Kimberly. She arrived ten minutes later, and I told her about my hospital stay.

"He was responsible for giving you a concussion. We can really make him pay for that. We are going to ask for one hundred thousand dollars for you to not file charges, and we can also get more money from the firm. I got an alert about the media talking about the incident."

"I know. I want my name to be kept out of it." I had flashbacks to how the media hounded me after my affair with Eugene went public. I knew it would be bad for me because the world hated women who brought down powerful men.

"Don't worry, we can work that out with them to keep your name out of it. I'm sure they want to keep this as quiet as possible because I know they don't want the negative attention now that they are representing another high-profile client. I'm still waiting on a word from my investigator to find out more about Carlos Dutton."

I was glad that she was close to finding out what was going on with Carlos because something just wasn't right with him. Kimberly went over the proposal with me, and then she took pictures of the bruises of my wrist on her cell phone and I took some photos too. I called Harrell to let him know that we were ready to speak with him.

I drove to the law firm with Kimberly following behind me. When we arrived, we went inside the building. The other employees eyed us as we walked down the halls with a purpose. We took the elevator to the second floor, and Harrell's assistant told me that they were waiting in the conference room for us. We walked down the long hall and around the corner and to the conference room. Harrell was there along with Carlos and another man that I didn't recognize.

"Good morning, gentlemen. I am Kimberly Lanier, and I'm here to represent Miss Murray," Kimberly said as we joined them at the conference table.

I spoke to them, careful not to look at Carlos, who had a deep frown on his face.

"I'll get right to it. Mr. Dutton physically assaulted my client leaving bruises on her wrists and caused her to have a concussion." Kimberly took the paperwork about my hospital stay out of her briefcase and slid it across the table for them to look at it. Next, she showed them my bruises on her cell phone.

Kimberly and I watched silently as the three men looked at all the evidence in front of them.

The man I didn't recognize spoke up. "My name is Clinton Henderson, and I am representing Mr. Dutton as well as the firm. What kind of offer would you like?" he asked.

"I'm glad you asked," Kimberly said. "We would like one hundred thousand from Mr. Dutton, so Miss Murray will not press charges and also another two hundred thousand from the firm. Her name will not be released to the public, and all parties will agree not to talk about this incident with anyone."

Clinton nodded his head and then looked at Harrell and Carlos for their approval. They agreed with the terms. Kimberly handed them the proposal that stated that Carlos would pay me ten thousand dollars a month until the hundred thousand dollars was paid in full, and the law firm would pay me twenty thousand dollars a month until the two hundred thousand dollars was paid in full. We all signed the agreement, and I informed them that I wouldn't be coming back. Carlos abruptly stood up, catching everyone off guard, and then left the conference room furious, slamming the door behind him. After he left, we all looked at each other shocked at his attitude.

"Sorry about that," Harrell apologized. "Carlos is upset because he is being replaced by Clinton here. We will be announcing in the morning that Dutton and Harrell will now be called Harrell and Henderson."

I wasn't that surprised about Carlos being fired because his actions had been made public. I knew that they didn't need that negative attention, especially when they were trying to get their client off on a rape charge. Kimberly and I shook their hands and then left the building.

Once we exited the building, Kimberly's cell phone rung. She answered it, and I watched as a grave look came across his face. "Okay, thanks for letting me know," she said and then ended the call. She put her phone back in her purse, and then she slowly looked up at me.

"What is it?" I asked, already bracing myself for the bad news.

"That was my private investigator. He told me that Carlos suffers from bipolar disorder. He said that he got someone to unseal a juvenile file when Carlos was fifteen. He was attacking his girlfriend, and when his sister tried to step in, he attacked her too. His girlfriend suffered a broken eye socket, and his sister had broken ribs and collar bone. He was arrested, but they determined that he needed help. He had stopped taking his medication. He was sent to a hospital for a while until he started taking his medication again."

Her words caused a chill to go down my spine. Now I understood his mood swings, and why he had become so fixated on me so quickly.

Kim gave me a worried look. "He most likely stopped taking his medication again. You really need to be careful, Felicia, because it looks like you got into it with the wrong guy. Now that he's been let go from his job, he's probably going to be on a rampage. The way he left the conference room indicated that."

"Please stop it, Kimberly. You're not helping me. In fact, you're scaring me." I said, irritated.

"I'm sorry. I'm not trying to scare you. Just be careful, that's all."

"I know. Didn't mean to snap at you. This situation is just getting to me."

"Don't stress yourself out about it. You should go home and get some rest."

"I will and thanks for everything. I'll send you a check in the morning," I said, and we crossed the street and went to our cars.

I sat there in my car for a moment and watched as Kimberly pulled out of the parking lot. I needed to take a moment to gather myself. All this was a lot to take in. Yes, I won another case, but I had been physically assaulted and angered a potentially dangerous man. So, did I really win after all?

Chapter 8

For the next week, I stayed in the house and rested just like the doctor told me. I felt better physically, and my bruises had faded. During this time, I had a lot of time to think about everything. Latrice called me and asked me if I was okay because she figured I was the assistant that got assaulted. I told her everything that happened and to say she was worried was an understatement. She gave me a lecture about how I was living my life. Instead of being defensive, I listened to her. It was a frightening ordeal. I never expected to get attacked like that. I didn't tell her about Carlos' mental state because that would probably raise her blood pressure. I had to admit to myself that I didn't want to do this anymore. I just wanted to get a job and work without setting men up. I would start looking for a job in a couple of weeks and hopefully put this all behind me.

I was still very worried about the situation. I hadn't heard anything from Carlos, and that was good. I watched Harrell give a press conference saying that Carlos had been relieved of his duties, and he was now bringing Clinton Henderson in. The crowd asked question after question, and they tried hard to get Harrell to tell them the name of the victim. I had to hold my breath as I waited for what Harrell had to say, but of course, he didn't reveal my name. I knew it was going to be hard for Carlos to get another job and earn his respect back.

I had to admit that I felt guilty, and that's something that I never felt before after a victory. On top of the guilt, I was feeling anxious, scared and I also hadn't been sleeping well. I decided to go to the gym to work off all this energy that I had.

Once I arrived at the gym, I brought my bag inside and headed to the equipment. I decided to get on the treadmill. I adjusted the machine to the speed I desired and begin running on the treadmill. I could feel the tension slowly leave my body as I ran. I had been running for a few minutes when a handsome man got on the machine beside me. He had a lean fit body, and I could tell he worked out quite often. He had a nice chestnut brown complexion and was a little over six feet tall. He wore his hair cut close, and his beard and mustache was neatly trimmed. He noticed me looking him over and smiled at me. I smiled back, feeling a little embarrassed. He set the machine up and begin running on the machine.

A few minutes later, I left the machine and went to sit in the corner on the bench. I took a bottle of water out of my bag and took a sip. I was surprised to see the handsome gentleman walking towards me. He sat beside me and wiped his face with a towel.

"I'm Kelvin. What's your name?" he asked politely.

"Felicia."

"Well, Miss Felicia, I couldn't help but notice you. I was wondering if you would like to have dinner with me sometime."

"Dinner, are you serious?" I asked, shocked that he asked me out.

"Sure, why not?"

"Well, you don't even know me, so why do you want to have dinner with me?" I asked skeptically. He was a walking image of perfection to me, so it seemed too good to be true that he wanted to go out with me.

He laughed lightly. "I like what I see, and I want to go out with you to get to know you."

I couldn't help but smile at him. *Smooth,* I thought. I was very attracted to him, but with all that I had just went though, I didn't know if now was a good time.

"Now is not a good time for me. I have a lot on my plate right now," I said.

A disappointed look came across his face. "I understand, but there is probably always going to be something going on in your life. So why not go out with me and enjoy yourself?" he asked, not giving up.

I smiled inside. I liked his persistence. Who knew, maybe going out with him would bring some peace and joy in my life that I needed.

"Okay, I'll go out with you."

"Great, how about this weekend?"

Sounds perfect. We exchanged numbers, and we talked for a few more minutes until Kelvin left, saying he had to go to work. He was a Radiologist at the hospital nearby.

After he left, I had to admit that I felt a lot better. I worked for another hour, took a shower in one of the bathrooms at the gym, changed clothes, and then I drove home.

Once home, I went to unlock my door, but discovered that it was already unlocked. I was immediately alarmed and slowly entered my condo. My mouth dropped open when I walked into the living room and saw that my fifty-five-inch flat screen tv was cracked. Lying in front of it was a broken vase. Someone had obviously thrown a vase at it. I could smell a strong bleach odor in my condo. I walked into the kitchen and discovered that all of the beverages in the fridge had been poured out on the floor. My head started pounding and my heart started racing. I wondered what else I would discover.

I walked into my bedroom, and the bleach odor got stronger. My eyes got watery, and I started feeling nauseous from the strong odor. My walk-in closet was empty except my shoes. I went into the bathroom and saw all my clothes were in the tub filled with bleach. All my clothes were ruined. I started gagging, and I knew I needed to leave my condo. I quickly left my condo, drove to a nearby hotel, and booked a room for two nights. Once inside my room, I sat on my bed. I knew this was Carlos' doing. How did he know where I lived? I had so many questions that I needed answers to. How was he able to get past the doorman? I knew I needed to call the police and report this, but I was scared to. Plus, I had no proof that Carlos did this.

I laid back on the bed and stared at the ceiling. I was hoping that Carlos had gotten all his anger out of his system and would hopefully leave me alone now. But as I stared up at the ceiling, I knew it was wishful thinking.

Chapter 9

Kelvin

I left the gym in a good mood. I had gotten the number of a beautiful woman, and she agreed to go out with me. I was really looking forward to it. No woman had gotten me this excited since Gabrielle. Gabrielle and I had broken up about five years ago, but we started dating seven years ago. I was a radiologist, and Gabrielle was a pediatric surgeon. We were both residents at the time. I was always at the hospital, so quite naturally, I would date doctors or nurses. Gabrielle and I hit it off. I loved her beautiful golden skin and light brown eyes. She was sweet and compassionate, so she was perfect for operating on kids and putting them and their parents at ease.

I asked her to marry me, and I thought everything was perfect until our wedding day. As she stood in front of me, she started crying. I asked her what was troubling her because she was scaring everyone in our building because her crying wasn't a happy cry like when you shed happy tears on your wedding day. It was a painful cry. She revealed to me that she had slept with my best man, who happened to be my best friend, Darius. I stood there shocked as she told me this. Everyone gasped, and the minister kept nervously looking at the both of us, not knowing what to do. I turned around and looked at Darius. He started to apologize, but I silenced him by punching him in the mouth. I started attacking him right there at the altar. Luckily, the guests were able to break it up.

I left that church, broken and angry. Gabrielle tried to apologize, telling me that she loved me and made a mistake, but I wasn't trying to hear it. She had slept with my best friend the night before. Instead of pulling me aside and talking to me in private, she confessed in front of all our friends and family. I told her I didn't want to see her ever again. She kept trying to get me back, but she transferred to another hospital when she saw it wasn't happening. A year later, she married Darius. That just let me know that she couldn't have been that sorry or serious about getting me back if she went off and married Darius. I went and talked to Darius after I learned of their engagement because I knew it had to be more to it. The way Gabrielle explained it, it was a one-time thing. But Darius told me that he and Gabrielle had developed feelings for each other. He said that they didn't do anything but kiss until the night before the wedding when they couldn't hold back their feelings any longer. It hurt me to hear that because Gabrielle had fallen in love with him.

He apologized, and there was nothing else I could do but leave. I forgave them, but the pain and hurt took a long time to fade. I wasn't friends with them anymore. I hadn't talked to Darius since the day he explained everything to me. My parents had told me that they had moved to Los Angeles.

I dated some since then, but I never felt a spark with anyone until today. The moment I laid eyes on Felicia, she had my attention. I saw the way she was looking at me, and I knew she felt the same way. I watched her out of the corner of my eye as she ran on the treadmill. Her body was great, and she seemed nice, but definitely guarded. There was a story there, and I was looking forward to knowing what it was. She intrigued me.

My parents would be happy to know that I was going out on a date with someone I was really looking forward to getting to know. I grew up in Las Vegas. My parents Oscar and Lucinda Harris, were heavily into the church and raised my brother and me as Christians. My father is a landscaper and started his own business, which was very successful. My mother made a living as a substitute teacher. My father's business and as well as academic scholarships got me through college and medical school. I made straight A's and graduated from college and medical school with honors. I am now forty-two, and my younger brother Randall, who is thirty-five, is a successful graphic artist. Our parents were proud of both of us.

I was on my way to work now to start my day, and meeting Felicia this morning made my day brighter.

Chapter 10

Kelvin

It was Saturday night, and I was in a booth at a nice Five-star restaurant, waiting for Felicia to arrive. I offered to pick her up, but she told me she wanted to meet me at the restaurant. I could understand that she wasn't comfortable with me picking her up at her house. She didn't know me that well yet. I had talked to her a few times over the week, but she didn't talk to me long, and she seemed distracted. Something seemed to be going on with her, but I was hoping she would open up to me some tonight. I talked to my mother earlier, and she wanted me to come over for dinner tonight. I told her I couldn't because I had plans. I didn't want to tell my mother I was going out on a date because every time I did, she would get excited, hoping I would find the right one. She was ready to be a grandmother and counted on me to make that happen first because Randall liked to play the field and wasn't serious about anyone yet. After she hounded me, I finally told her I met a nice woman, and we were going out tonight. She was already asking to meet her. We would see how things went.

I looked up to see Felicia walking towards me. She looked lovely in a sapphire blue, knee-length dress. She had her hair out, and it fell past her shoulders. When she arrived at the booth, I stood up, kissed her on the cheek, and then we sat down.

"You look gorgeous," I told her.

"Thank you. You look handsome."

"Thank you," I said. I made sure I looked decent tonight in Versace.

The waitress came to our table and took our orders. We took a moment to look at the food choices and decided on the gourmet lobster dinner and lemonade to drink.

"I'm happy you joined me tonight. So how was your week?" I asked to get her talking.

She hesitated, "It was fine."

I studied her for a minute. I knew often when people said it was fine, they usually mean the opposite. "How was work?" I asked, realizing that I didn't know what kind of job she had.

A sheepish look appeared on her face. "Well, I'm currently not working, but I'm going to start looking for jobs next week."

So that was what was wrong. She was currently unemployed and obviously embarrassed by it. "What kind of work are you looking for because maybe I could help?"

"Well, I have a lot of administrative experience," she said.

"Okay, I'll see if there are any positions at the hospital."

Her face lit up. "You would do that?"

"Yes, it will be no problem."

"Thanks, I appreciate that."

The waitress brought our food and drinks to us, and we began eating. "So, do you go to church?" I asked her.

Felicia looked uncomfortable. "I used to, but I don't go that much anymore."

"Okay, I'm a Christian and go to church as often as I can. Sometimes my job as a radiologist can cause me to miss church, but you should come to church with me sometimes. I go to Greater Baptist Church."

"I'll think about it," she said.

Felicia and I talked and enjoyed our meal. I learned that she was thirty years old. She was over ten years younger than me, but I didn't mind at all. Felicia began to relax and enjoy herself, telling me she grew up in Arkansas and hadn't been in Las Vegas that long. We ordered an Oreo pie for dessert.

I felt like I knew her a little better, but it seemed as if it was something she was holding back. Maybe she would tell me in time.

Chapter 11

Felicia

After a nice dinner with Kelvin, I drove home in a much better mood. After spending the night in the hotel after Carlos had broken into my apartment, I went home and cleaned up the mess. The bleach smell still lingered in my condo. I went shopping, replacing most of my clothes and my flat screen tv. I had changed my locks and got an alarm system installed. I had been a nervous wreck all week looking over my shoulder. I wanted my life to go back to normal. Meeting Kelvin was great. He was so nice to me, and I could see myself getting serious about him. He was older and mature, which was a good thing in his case. Eugene was older than me, and that turned out bad. I hadn't wanted to get serious about a guy since Eugene. I could see that Kelvin cared about my well-being because he offered to help me get a job, but now that I thought about it. I didn't think it would be a good idea if we worked at the same place. I would look online and see what jobs were available. I had only worked in administrative positions, but it shouldn't be too hard to find another job in that field. I would normally leave the city or state after I won a suit, but I liked Las Vegas, and Kelvin was giving me more reasons to want to stay here.

When I arrived home, I turned off the beeping alarm and then went to take a shower. After taking a shower, I watched tv, but my mind was distracted with thoughts of Kelvin. He was good for me, but it was a lot he didn't know about me. I wondered how he would react if he knew I had an affair with a high-profile pastor, and then aborted his baby, only to start setting up men to harass me so I could file a suit against them. He would run so far away from me. I could see that he had a good relationship with God, and I wondered if I could recommit myself to God. I could never tell him these things about me, and I could only hope that he would never find out about it. As I lay there thinking about Kelvin, I fell asleep.

I awakened to a body on top of me. I opened my mouth to scream, but a hand was put over my mouth. It was dark in the room, so I was trying to make out the face on top of me.

"You think you can play games with me, but when I want to collect on your offer you want to file charges against me and take my money." Carlos whispered harshly in my ear, then he put a knife to my throat. I could smell the alcohol on his breath.

I body was wracked with a gripping fear. I closed my eyes for a minute then reopened them, hoping it was a nightmare, but it wasn't, Carlos was indeed on top of me breathing heavily in my ear with a knife to my throat. I wondered how he got into my condo again after I had the locks changed and an alarm system, and then I remembered I forgot to reset the alarm. I was hoping that mistake wouldn't cost me my life.

"I'm going to take my hand off your mouth and when I do you better not scream. Because if you do I'm going to stab you in the throat then you won't be able to scream again. You understand?"

I nodded my head and he removed his hand from my mouth. "Why are you doing this?" I asked slowly scared if I talked too fast the blade would cut my throat.

"You know why I'm doing this." Carlos spat out and pushed the knife harder against my throat. It stung, and I knew I was cut. "You wanted to play games with me to trick me out of my money. I could take what I want from you right now, but you know what I don't want you anymore because you disgust me with all your trickery.

"Please don't hurt me," I begged as tears began to trickle down my face.

Carlos laughed insanely. "That's just what I want; to have you at my mercy. You destroyed my reputation and my career."

"I'm sorry about that, but you need help. You need to get back on your medication."

Carlos was quiet for a moment, and then he started yelling. "What do you know about what kind of medications I take? Who are you *really*?"

"Listen, I know you suffer from bipolar disorder."

"Shut up! You don't know a thing about me!" Carlos yelled and slapped me hard across the face."

My face stung from the slap, and I knew I had to choose my words carefully. "Leave now, and I won't tell the cops anything about this," I said as calmly as I could. My face was aching, and I was going crazy inside.

"I don't care about the cops. I enjoy tormenting you. I looked in your closet and saw that you replaced all your clothes already, and my check won't be delivered to you until next week. You have this nice place and car. You have a lot of money already, so why do you need mine? I tell you why because you're an evil, greedy slut that I should never have hired."

His insults hurt and all I could do is look up in his face knowing he had all the control. If I attempted to move, he would jam that knife in my neck, and that's not how I wanted to leave this world.

"But this isn't over. I'm going to make your life miserable. I have connections so I can find any information about you that I want, and I can always get inside your apartment. I have my ways." Carlos said mysteriously and got up and slowly backed out of my room.

I heard my door close a moment later and I felt relieved that he didn't kill me, but would I be so lucky next time? I laid there on my bed for a while in shock trying to come to terms with what just happened to me. He wasn't going to stop. I knew I should call the police, but I didn't want to bring any attention to myself. I didn't want anyone to know I was the woman that Carlos Dutton assaulted because people were still curious about it. Even if I called the police and told them what happened he would keep coming after me. I wasn't going to feel completely safe no matter what I did.

Finally, I slowly got out of bed and went downstairs and checked the lock on my door, and just like last time it didn't look like it had been tampered with. He said he had his ways of getting into my apartment, but my guess was he was excellent at picking locks. I then went upstairs and into my bathroom and turned on the light. My neck was bleeding from the puncture wound from the knife and there was a purple bruise on my cheek. My eyes were red and swollen. I looked horrible and tried to think of what to do. I felt like I deserved all this because of what I did to him and all the other men.

I cleaned my neck up and put some alcohol on it. I put a band aid on it then went back into my room and curled up on my bed in a fetal position and cried myself to sleep.

Chapter 12

Felicia

I woke up the next morning feeling miserable. My body was sore from Carlos being pressed on top of me. I did have a clearer idea of how I should handle the situation. It was a little farfetched and could potentially make the situation worse, but I had to try. I was going to speak with Carlos's wife Mindy. She probably was the only one who could get through to him. But I wonder if she was watching out for him the way she should because he was at my house last night, and I wonder if she even knew he was missing.

I got my tablet and looked up her Facebook profile. A lot of people put their whole lives on Facebook, and I wondered if Mindy was one of those people. I looked up Mindy Dutton, and there she was. She had a beautiful profile picture up. She had pictures of their son and pictures of her and Carlos as well. Looking at the pictures would make you think they were the perfect couple, but the world knew differently now.

As I studied her profile, I saw that she sold and did make-up at her home. I thought it was cool that she had her own make-up line. So this is what Carlos meant when he said his wife had a hobby. I don't think he was giving her enough credit. She even posted pictures of the make-up jobs she did. I must say that she did a very good job. She had a phone number listed for anyone that wanted her services.

I wasted no time calling the number. "Hi, Mindy speaking

how can I help you." She said in a professional voice.

"Hi this is Celine Thomas and I wanted a make-up job done. I have a special night planned and I want to look my best."

"Great, I have some time this afternoon at about 1:00. I can come by your house if that's okay with you."

I had to think quickly. I didn't want her to come to my condo. "Would it be okay if I meet at your house?" I knew I was taking a risk of Carlos being home. I just had to hope he wasn't there.

"That will be fine. My husband will actually be away for a few hours today. So that will be a perfect time," she said with a laugh.

She told me her address, and we agreed to meet at 1:00. We ended the call, and I went to go take a shower. As the water beat down on my body, I thought about how insane all this was. I didn't know how Mindy was going to react once she opened the door and recognized me from the law firm, but I just had to go with it.

When I got out of the shower, I dressed comfortably in a pair of jeans and a simple blouse. I went to the mirror and saw that my bruise had gotten darker, and my cheek was slightly swollen. Carlos had hit me pretty hard. I covered up my bruise the best I could with makeup and then I heard my phone chirp and went to go look at it and discovered I had a text message from Kelvin.

It read I'm taking a quick break at work, and I wanted to let you know I had a wonderful time with you last night. Looking forward to going out with you again soon. I'm working late tonight, so I will try to call you sometime tomorrow to set up a time to meet again. Looking forward to seeing you.

I closed my eyes and let out a sigh. Kelvin sent me this thoughtful message, and I hadn't thought about him at all this morning. I had so much other things going on. Here this wonderful man had come into my life and I couldn't enjoy him like I should because of the awful things I had done had come back to bite me in a major way. I thought about texting him back and telling him that I couldn't go out with him anymore. He was a good guy and I was probably going to ruin his life. I had a mentally ill man harassing me. How ironic I wanted to be harassed but not like this. I never in a million years would think things would turn around on me like this. I was just about to text Kelvin, but something wouldn't let me go through with it. I was emotional now and didn't want to make any irrational decisions. I would see how things went with Mindy, and then I would decide if I should go out with Kelvin again.

I went to the kitchen and had toast and eggs. I managed eat it, but I really didn't have much of an appetite. I busied myself by looking at jobs online until it was time to go see Mindy.

I left my condo and stopped in the lobby to talk to the doorman Andrew. "Hey Andrew, did you see anyone suspicious come into the lobby last night?"

A confused look came across Andrew's face. "No, I didn't see anyone suspicious come in. Did something happen? Are you okay?" Andrew asked as he looked at my face and then lowered his eyes to my neck that was bandaged.

"No, I'm okay. I was just asking. Thought I heard some unusual noise in the building last night, is all. Thank you," I said and quickly walked away and left the building. I'm not sure if Andrew believed me, but I could only hope he did.

I drove to Mindy's house and pulled into the driveway of the huge two-level home. A gold Lexus was in the driveway and I assumed it belonged to Mindy. I pulled in behind her Lexus, exited my car and walked up to the house feeling anxious.

I rang the doorbell and Mindy answered it a moment later looking nice in a fuchsia V-neck blouse and jean skirt. "Hi." She said and then her mouth dropped open once she recognized me. "You? What are you doing here?" she asked with a frown.

"I need to talk to you about Carlos."

"You don't need to tell me anything about my husband, now leave." She said and tried to shut the door, but I put my foot in the door to stop her. "Do you want me to call the police?"

"It's important. Carlos came to my house last night and put a knife to my neck."

That got Mindy's attention. Her eyes went to the band aid on my neck. "Okay, come in, but you better not try anything funny." She warned.

She stepped aside and allowed me to enter and shut the door behind me once I was inside. I followed her into the huge living room, and we took a seat on her black and white sectional sofa.

"I'm sorry I called you and pretended to be someone else, but Carlos has been harassing me. He broke into my home and I'm very afraid; look what he did to my neck. He hit me in the face, and I had to cover my face with make-up. He also destroyed my tv and bleached all my clothes. I know Carlos suffers from bipolar disorder and you need to get him some help before things turn deadly."

"Carlos stopped taking his meds three weeks ago, and when he doesn't his behavior can become very eccentric, and he usually drink to try to cope and that only makes things worse. He can become very hypersexual when he's off his meds and you flirting and teasing him didn't help matters. He's become fixated on you, and it's going to be hard for him to stop now. I've tried to get him to get back on his meds but he won't listen to me. He's out right now looking for another job, but he doesn't need to be working right now. He should focus on getting better. I'm really all his has because his family isn't much help when he gets like this."

"Maybe you should have him committed if he won't take his meds."

A scowl appeared on Mindy's face. "I'm not having my husband committed. He will be fine. I just have to convince him to get back on his meds."

"Well you need to make sure that happens. Because the next time he breaks into my home I'm going to file a restraining order on him."

"You have some nerve coming in here threatening to press charges against my husband. You're already getting a hundred thousand dollars out of him." Mindy spat out angrily.

"Look I'm sorry, but I have to think about my safety."

"You said what you have to say, now please leave my home and don't come back here again. And the fact that you pretended to be someone else to get into my home proves that you have some issues too. If you come here again or call me, I will file a restraining order against you."

"Understood," I said and left their house.

I quickly got into my car and drove down the street and away from their house. Things went better than I expected. I was hoping she could get through to Carlos, because if she didn't, I didn't know what I was going to do.

Chapter 13

Kelvin

A month past and things were going well between Felicia and me. We've been spending time together whenever we could. We worked out at the gym together, but I could still sense that she wasn't telling me everything about herself. She was a mystery to me. A month ago, she had a huge bruise on her check and a cut on her neck. She told me that she got into a fight with one of her jealous neighbors. Her explanation seemed to be a bit odd, but Felicia is a beautiful woman and I know how petty and catty females can be. But my gut was telling me that something was off about her story. I told her about what Gabrielle did to me on my wedding day in hopes that should would open up to me, but she didn't. I was going to be patient with her because I liked her a lot, and if she wasn't being truthful with me it would reveal itself eventually. She met my parents and brother and they liked her. My parents said she was a bit guarded, and I couldn't disagree with them on that. Felicia started a new job two weeks ago as a receptionist at a dentist office.

The good thing is that today Felicia was finally going to go to church with me. I knew she would enjoy herself because Pastor Samuel Bell was excellent, and I hope she got a good word today. I could tell she was nervous as we walked into the huge church. The usher seated us, and we stood and listened to the praise music. I clapped my hands as I listened to the music. I looked over at Felicia and she glanced around nervously like she felt out of place.

"Just relax, you belong here just like everyone else." I whispered in her ear.

She gave me a small smile and it seemed as if she started to relax a little. The music played for another fifteen minutes and then Pastor Bell came to the podium and we took our seats.

"Good morning." He greeted. The crowd said good morning in unison. "I hope you came to get a good word today because today I wanted to talk to you about letting go of past sins and hurts. Many people stay trapped in the past because of sins they committed and how they've been hurt in the past. If you don't deal with it properly it can turn you into someone you never thought you'd be and, that can only hurt you in the long run. When you sin it is important to repent and give it to God no matter what it is. 1John 1:9 reads, If we confess our sins, he is faithful and just to forgive us of our sins and to cleanse us from all unrighteousness. Ephesians 1:7 reads, In him we have redemption through his blood, the forgiveness of our trespasses, according to the riches of his grace. See God will wipe your slate clean after you sin. God is not like man. Man will often remind you of the things you done in your past, but God is not like that. He will forgive you. So, don't let the guilt and embarrassment of past sins hold you back and trick you into thinking there is nothing else better for you.

"Next I want to talk to you about dealing with a broken heart. If you've been hurt like you never imagined you don't have to carry all that around with you. Give it to God. 1Peter 5:7 reads, Cast all your anxiety on him because he cares for you. 2Corinthians 12:9 reads, But, he said to me, "My grace is sufficient for you, for my power is made perfect in weakness." Therefore, I will boast all the more gladly about my weakness, so that Christ's power may rest on me.

"God wants the best for you and for you to live your best life. He knew we would mess up, but He will be there to pick us up. You don't have to walk around angry or go around hurting other people because you've been hurt. You don't go around hiding things about yourself because you are embarrassed about things from your past. Let it all go and give it to God. Now, let's bow our heads and pray."

Before I bowed my head to pray I looked over at Felicia and saw that she was crying. That was a powerful word, and I could feel God's presence strongly in the building. Hopefully now she could find some peace with whatever she was dealing with.

After the service, Felicia and I went to my house. We were going to cook Sunday dinner together. Felicia was putting together the macaroni and cheese casserole and I was seasoning the chicken. I glanced over at her as she worked. She seemed to have gathered herself a little, but I wanted to know what made her cry.

"That was a good word today wasn't it?" I asked her.

"Yes, it was. I didn't realize how much I missed church until today."

"Why did you leave the church?" I asked her.

"I rather not talk about it."

I studied her for a moment wondering why she was so closed off. "Look, you know you can talk to me about anything and I won't judge you."

"I appreciate that, but it's some things that I just don't like to talk about."

"I know, but if we're going to make this work, I need for you to be more open with me. I need to know why you don't care to visit your parents, and I would eventually like to know why you left church in the first place." After she met my parents, I asked her about meeting her family and she was against it saying that she wasn't close to them anymore.

"I like it that you care so much, but I'm not ready to talk about any of that." She said in a voice that let me know that she was done with the subject.

We finished making dinner in silence and when it was done. I lightened the mood by asking her about work and talking about our favorite shows we liked to watch. After we finished eating we went into the den to watch television.

I powered the tv on and it was turned to CNN. They went to

breaking news. "Hi I'm Andy Steel and I have breaking news about the Alton Brewer case. After further investigation, the police found evidence that pointed to the security guard Randy Jenkins. After interviewing neighbors they learned that he was borderline obsessed with Julia Neil and would often harass her male companions. It is believed that Mr. Jenkins became jealous after Alton visited Miss Neil, and he went in and beat her after Alton left. After searching his apartment, they found bloody clothes in his apartment that matches Miss Neil's blood. We are told that the charges against Alton Brewer have been dropped. As you know this case has become even more high-profile after Carlos Dutton was fired for assaulting his assistant. I will now take you to a live press conference." They then went to a press conference being held by Earl Harrell and Clinton Henderson. You could tell they and Alton Brewer were ecstatic as they answered questions from the crowd.

"Wow, he actually didn't do it. I was really thinking that he did. Who knew that Julia Neil was being stalked by a crazy security guard," I said and let out a light chuckle.

"A woman being stalked and beaten is nothing to laugh at," Felicia said angrily. Her beautiful face had a huge frown on it.

"Whoa, I didn't mean anything by that. I'm just surprised that Alton do it. That's all."

She didn't say anything. She just kept frowning at me.

"Okay, maybe it was distasteful for me to laugh, and I'm sorry I upset you," I said, wondering where her sudden outburst was coming from.

"It's just that everyone is so happy for Alton Brewer, but they are not thinking about the woman that was hurt," she said, still not letting it go.

"I think people are concerned about her, and that security guard is in jail where he belongs," I said and then turned the channel. I desperately wanted to get off this subject.

I found a movie for us to watch and I put my arm around Felicia as we watched the movie. I could feel her relaxing in my arms, but I couldn't totally relax because I was still thinking about her strange, unexpected outburst.

Chapter 14

Felicia

The next morning, I was sitting behind the desk at work watching some of the patients fill out the dental forms. Last night was a close call. I knew Kelvin knew something was up with me after I snapped at him about him laughing at Julia being stalked. He was so patient and caring and I just didn't want to burden him with what I had been through recently. I was hoping it was all behind me now because I hadn't heard from Carlos. Hopefully his wife got him some help.

I was happy that I found another job, but I feel as if I should be doing more with my life. I had been so focused on setting men up to harass me, that I hadn't pursued a higher education. Working these administration jobs were cool, but I know I could do more. But the thing was I didn't know exactly what I wanted to be. I would look up some college courses online and decide what I wanted to major in.

The phone rang, and I set up a dental appointment and took the forms from the patients that were waiting. A few hours passed by, and it was now time for me to take a lunch break. I left out of the dental office and headed to my car. I hit the unlock button on my key ring, and I was about to open the door when I felt something poke me in the back.

"You better not scream or do anything foolish, because I will shoot you right in the back," Carlos said.

I froze. How did he know where I work? Then I remembered Carlos could find out about anything according to him.

"Open the door and get inside," he demanded.

Afraid for my life, I opened the door and got inside. Carlos hurried around to the passenger side and got in. I stared at Carlos, waiting for his next move. I was shocked by his appearance. His beard had grown out and he had dark circles under his eyes.

"Start the car now," Carlos demanded and pointed the gun at me.

I looked around, hoping that a patient would leave out the building or pull up, but no one was outside at the moment.

"Stop looking around and start the car now," Carlos whispered harshly. I started the car, and Carlos typed an address into my GPS system. "Drive to this location."

I pulled out of the parking lot and on the highway. "Why are you still harassing me?" I asked in a nervous voice.

Carlos let out a loud laugh. "After you paid my wife a visit, I wanted to go after you, but my wife begged me not to. I started back taking my medication for my wife because she stood by me through all of this, and it only makes me love her more. But I stopped taking my medication a week ago, and then I saw the press conference that Harrell and Henderson gave. I watched them get the victory last night, and all I could think about is that it should have been me. You ruined my career and reputation. No one wants to hire me for anything because of you. My bank account is dwindling, and you should pay the ultimate price."

My heart started beating so fast that I thought it would beat out of my chest.

"I'm going to get rid of you once and for all when we get to this location."

I didn't want my life to end like this. I knew I would be dead if I drove to that location. I had to will my mind to think. My hands were shaking, and I gripped my hands on the stirring wheel so tight that they started to ache. How could I get myself out of this? *Think Felicia think?*

Then the answer came to me. It was risky, but it was the only way that I could possibly get out of this alive, but it could also kill me, but I had to do it. I increased the speed of the car and jerked the car hard to the left. The car overcorrected and flipped a few times before coming to a stop.

We were upside down and I looked over at Carlos and he was unconscious. My body was aching, and I felt like I couldn't breathe. I looked down at my shirt and it was covered in blood. I was feeling weak and dizzy and then I lost conscious.

Chapter 15

Felicia

I slowly opened my eyes and the first face I see is Kelvin, and he had a worried look on his face. I look around wondering where I was. Then I remember the accident. Thank God I was alive. I looked at Kelvin and he had his white doctor's coat on.

Kelvin kissed me on top of the forehead. "I'm glad you are awake. You've been unconscious for a few hours. The police called me about your accident because I was the last number you dialed in the phone. I was already here at work, so I was able to come right in here and see you. I'm going to go get Dr. Hill, he's excellent, and you couldn't be in more capable hands," he said and left the room.

My head was aching, and I noticed my arm was in a case. A few minutes later, a middle-aged Caucasian man entered the room with Kelvin behind him.

"Hi, I'm Dr. Hill. You've been out for four hours. You suffered a punctured lung, you broke your arm, and you have a concussion. We are a little concerned about your concussion because you were admitted here for a concussion about a month ago, so we definitely want to monitor you. We were able to repair your lung, and there will be no permanent damage. It's going to take you about eight to ten weeks to fully recover."

Dr. Hill paused for a moment and looked at Kelvin. Kelvin was looking at me with a confused expression on his face. He probably was wondering about my previous concussion.

"There was another passenger in your car, Carlos Dutton, and he has a broken back. The police are waiting to talk to you because a loaded gun was found in the car. They were just curious about what was going on because his wife had some questions. Wait right here, I'll go get the officer," he said.

Kelvin walked closer to my bed. "I didn't want to say anything until the doctor talked to you, but I need to know what is going on, Felicia. Why were you riding around with Carlos Dutton? This doesn't make sense unless....." He stopped talking and squinted his eyes at me.

"It's not what you think," I tried to explain. Kelvin was about to say something else, but the police officer came in.

"Hi, I'm Officer McNeil, and I have some questions for you. We need to know what happened leading up to the accident. The gun found in the car with you and Mr. Dutton makes us think that something was going on. Mr. Dutton admitted it was his gun, but he refuses to say anything else, and I need you to tell me exactly what happened."

I looked at Kelvin, who was waiting anxiously for my answer then I looked back at the officer. I wanted to lie, but I knew I couldn't. Carlos had tried to kidnap and kill me at my job, and I couldn't keep this a secret any longer.

"Carlos kidnapped me from my job, holding me at gunpoint and forced me to drive to a location where he said he was going to kill me. I caused the accident to keep that from happening," I confessed, and tears began to stream down my face.

"What? Why didn't you tell me any of this?" Kelvin asked and stood up with a pained look on his face.

"Sir, I really need to get the story from her. Just relax," The officer said.

Kelvin sat back down, and I told the officer everything that happened, starting with the assault at the job."

Officer McNeil wrote everything down and said. "Don't worry, you're safe now. Mr. Dutton will be arrested. Officer McNeil then gave me his card and told me that he would keep in touch with me because he will probably have more questions for me.

After he left, I braced myself for the questions that Kelvin would have for me. "So, this is what you're dealing with? You were the woman that Carlos Dutton assaulted? Why wouldn't you just tell me that? He could have killed you."

"I know," I said dumbly. I didn't know what else to say. There was way more to the story than that.

Kelvin squinted his eyes at me. "That's all you have to say, I know?"

"There is a lot you don't know," I said weakly. My body was in pain.

"Obviously. Look, you need your rest, and I have to get back to work. We can talk about this later," he said and exited the room.

I closed my eyes, knowing that my whole world was about to blow up, and there wasn't much I could do about it.

Chapter 16

Kelvin

I left out of Felicia's hospital room with so many questions on my mind that I thought my brain would explode. As I was walking through the lobby on my way to the elevators, I saw police officers talking to an Asian woman who was extremely upset, and I stopped walking to see what was going on.

"I'm telling you, officers Felicia Murray preyed on my husband. She's done this to other men. My husband looked into her past. I'm telling you there is more to this woman than you realize. She came to my house a few weeks ago pretending to be someone else," The woman said frantically.

This was Carlos Dutton's wife, and she had a lot to say about Felicia, but was it true? I didn't want to believe the things she was saying about Felicia, but it was most likely true. Not wanting to hear anything else, I left the lobby area and walked around the corner to the elevators. When they opened, I took the elevator to the third floor to my work station, but I didn't know how I was going to concentrate on work with all of this on my mind.

Once on the third floor, I walked into the lab and looked at the scans. I was interrupted when one of the nurses peeped her head in the doorway.

"Is it okay if I come in? I have some x-rays for you to look at."

"Sure, come in," I said.

She handed me the x-rays. "These are the ex-rays of a high

school point guard. The orthopedic surgeon seems to think there may be a fracture in his wrist that she can't see, and we wanted you to take a look at them. He really wants to play tonight because he says basketball scouts will be there."

I stood up and put the x-ray on the whiteboard. I studied them. As I studied the x-ray, Felicia popped in my mind. I shoved the thoughts of her out of my mind to concentrate on the x-ray. There was a faint fracture in his wrist.

I took the ex-ray off the whiteboard, then turned around and looked at the nurse. "There is a small fracture in his wrist, and it should heal on its own. But if he puts too much pressure on, it will create a bigger fracture, so I have to recommend that he doesn't play."

"Okay, he's going to be disappointed," she said, took the x-rays from me, and left the lab.

I hated that he would have to miss an important game tonight, but if he fractures his wrist anymore, it will be worse for him. My thoughts went back to Felicia, but I willed them away because I had a lot of scans, x-rays, and mammograms to go over.

After I got through a good portion of my work, I went down to the cafeteria to get something to eat. I thought about stopping by Felicia's room, but I didn't want to talk to her right now. Especially after hearing the things Carlos's wife said about her. Did she really pretend to be someone else, so she could talk to her? If she did, she had some serious issues, but hopefully, there was a reasonable explanation.

After eating lunch, I got through the rest of the day and headed home about 7:00. When I arrived home, I took a shower and then made me a sandwich and grabbed a cup of juice, and I went into the den to watch tv. I turned the tv to the news channel.

"Hello, I'm Tom Allen, and we just learned that Carlos Dutton was arrested today for allegedly kidnapping and threatening the life of Felicia Murray. He kidnapped her, and they were in an accident. Both are said to be in stable condition. We believe Felicia is the assistant he assaulted about a month ago. Apparently, he has been stalking her for a month. It is rumored that Carlos Dutton suffers from bipolar disorder

and has recently stopped taking his medication. His wife Mindy Dut-
ton will be giving a live interview from her home that will be aired at a
later hour."

I shook my head. I had to watch that interview with Mindy because I believed she held all the answers that I was searching for about Felicia. My cell phone rang. It was my brother Randall.

"Hey, man. Has Felicia woken up yet?" he asked.

I had called him and told him about the accident, and now I wish I hadn't. I didn't know what to tell him about everything that was going on, but then again, it was now public information

"Yes, she's in stable condition and should be fully healed in about ten weeks."

"That's good. I told mom and dad what happened. I'm sure they will be calling you soon."

"They probably will," I said.

"I'm glad she's okay, because I know how you feel about her," Randall said with a light laugh.

It was obvious to my family that I adored Felicia. I think I was in love with her, and thought she was the one for me, but now I'm not so sure.

"Yes, I have strong feelings for her," I said, not wanting to say I loved her yet.

"I know. I'm going to let you go now but call me if anything changes," he said, and we hung up.

It was obvious that he hadn't heard the news story yet or he would have been bombarding me with questions. My cell phone rang, and I saw it was my mother. I didn't answer it because I knew she wanted to ask me questions about Felicia and I was done talking about it for now.

I finished eating my sandwich and then went upstairs to my room and laid on my bed and turned the television to a tv show. I would watch it for now until Mindy Dutton's interview. I definitely wanted to see what she had to say.

Chapter 17

Felicia

The doctor and nurse came in to check on me. After the nurse gave me a dose of pain medication, I fell asleep watching the news channel, and when I woke up, the news was on. Mindy Dutton was about to give an interview, and I knew it wouldn't be good.

"Hi, I'm Sarah Ryan from MBS news, and with me, I have Mindy Dutton. She is the wife of Carlos Dutton, the famed attorney, who used to work at Dutton, and Harrell recently renamed Harrell and Henderson. As you know, Carlos Dutton was arrested earlier for kidnapping and threatening Felicia Murray, who we now know was the assistant that he assaulted. They were involved in an accident earlier. Both were injured but are in stable condition. Mindy Dutton would like to clear up some things about her husband Carlos. Mindy, let's hear your story."

"First, I would like to thank you for giving me this opportunity to tell my story. My husband suffers from bipolar disorder and he recently went off his meds. His illness was exacerbated with the stress of his heavy workload. Then you had Felicia Murray, his newly hired administrative assistant, throwing herself at him.

"Mrs. Dutton, are you blaming Miss Murray for what Carlos did to her?" Sarah asked, and I was glad she did because it seemed as if she was trying to blame all this on me.

"No, I'm not. Carlos chose to act on her advances and took things too far, but I want the world to know things about Felicia. Carlos looked

into her background and discovered she filed sexual harassment law-suits on at least five men over the past five years and received a sub-stantial amount of money."

"Wow, that seems like a pattern," Sarah said.

"It's most definitely a pattern. She gets a job as an administrative assistant to these powerful me, and then she preys on them. Felicia is a beautiful woman, so most men will take the bait. She also slept with Pastor Eugene Marks, the popular Pastor from Little Rock, Arkansas."

"This is a lot you're revealing here," Sarah said, in shock. My head was pounding from being exposed this way.

"Yes, it needs to be put out there. She preys on men, and I feel like she belongs in jail for that. She even pretended to be someone else so she could talk to me. She wanted me to know Carlos' behavior was getting out of control. I got him back on his meds, and he was doing good for a while, until he saw Harrell and Henderson get the victory for the Alton Brewer case. He's worked so hard to get to this point in his career only to have it taken away," Mindy paused for a minute, and a distraught look came over her face. "Carlos needs help, and now he will get the help he needs, but it's a shame he has to do it behind bars. I'm going to do everything in my power to see that he won't have to stay in jail long."

"I'm sorry to hear about that. Mental illness is serious, and I hope Carlos gets better," Sarah said.

"Hopefully, he will. It's women like Felicia that give women a bad name, and she needs help herself. She has made a living by being an ac-cuser. She has gotten six figures from all of the cases she's filed."

"Thank you for speaking with us, Mrs. Dutton. You have defin-itely shown us it's two sides to every story, and everything isn't always black and white. I hope everything works out for you and Carlos."

Sarah wrapped up the interview and they went to another segment. I was paralyzed by the relation that I was "the accuser." That's what my life had been about for the last five years, and I had been proud of it until things went bad with Carlos Dutton. Now the whole world knew. I felt sick to my stomach. Carlos had been arrested for kidnapping and threatening me. He had also done all these other horrible things to me, but I knew the world now saw Carlos as my victim. They were on his side, and I would get blamed for everything, the woman always does. I turned the tv off and closed my eyes, hoping sleep would come.

Chapter 18

Felicia

I woke up the next morning when a nurse walked into the room. "How are you doing this morning, Miss Murray?" she asked, but I could see that curious look in her eyes. I knew she heard about or seen the interview.

"I'm feeling okay. My body aches some," I said.

"Okay, before I give you more medicine, the doctor has to examine you again. Is there anything I can get you?" she asked, studying me.

I was thirsty, so I asked for a cup of water, and she left to go get it. I was ready to leave this hospital. I didn't need judgement from the people who were supposed to be taking care of me.

The nurse came back in the room a few minutes later, followed by the doctor, handing me a cup of water. I took a quick sip and sat the cup on the stand beside the bed. The doctor examined me and checked my wounds. He said my blood pressure was a little high, so he wanted to monitor it, and then the nurse gave me some pain medication. I knew my blood pressure was high after watching that interview last night.

I turned the tv on to a movie and powered on my cell phone. I saw I had missed calls from Latrice and my parents. I'm sure she saw the interview last night and knew I had been in an accident. I knew they were worried, but I know my parents wanted to talk to me about the things Mindy revealed. I didn't want to talk to them, so I sent them a text letting them know I was okay. That would have to do for now.

I tried to get into the movie to take my mind off everything, but it wasn't working. Then there was a knock on my room door.

"Come in," I said, figuring it was one of the nurses. I was shocked to see Kelvin walk through the door. But I shouldn't have been too shocked because he said he wanted some answers.

He had a grim look on his face, and I mentally tried to prepare myself for all of the uncomfortable questions he was about to ask me. He walked over and sat in the chair beside my hospital bed.

"How are you feeling, Felicia?" he asked me.

"Better. I'm still in pain, but I have to give the pain medication some more time to kick in."

"Is all the things Mindy said about you true?"

Here it was the moment I had been dreading. "Yes," I admitted.

A pained look came across Kelvin's face and he shook his head. "So, you racked up a bunch of money by getting men to harass you? That's how you have that nice car and apartment. Why would you do this?"

"After Pastor Eugene Marks abandoned me after our affair became public, it really hurt because the world blamed me more than him. He was the one in position of power, but not only that." I took a deep breath because I was about to admit something that really pained me to talk about. "Even after everything that happened, I still wanted to be with him, and he came back to me briefly. I became pregnant, but he wouldn't answer any of my calls, so I aborted the baby, and I regret it so much," I said and began crying.

Kelvin took my hand. "I know that must have hurt you, but you had to know what you were getting yourself into by having sex with a married man. That type of situation usually never ends well."

I snatched my hand from him. I didn't want to hear his judgement. "That was hard for me to tell you, so I expected a little more compassion."

"I am showing you compassion, but you have to take responsibility for the lies you told and the way you choose to live your life. Carlos could have killed you, and you didn't trust me enough to tell me the truth. If you didn't want to tell me, you should have told the cops. This all could have been avoided."

The truth of his words felt like needles stabbing my heart. I was laying in this bed, banged up, and my life exposed to the world because of all the things I had done.

Kelvin stood up. "Maybe if you told me all these things about yourself, I would have been prepared to deal with all this, but now I just can't. We're over. Take care of yourself," he said sadly but firmly and left the room.

The tears kept falling as I realized that I had lost such a wonderful man. Why didn't I just tell him the truth? I felt miserable, and I knew that there was nothing else left for me in Las Vegas.

Chapter 19

Felicia

It's four months later, and I'm back in Little Rock. After everything came out, I decided it was time for me to return to the city where I grew up. I couldn't run from my past pain anymore. I had been thinking a lot about what Latrice said about the heart of a sinner. My heart was broken, and until I dealt with what was causing me so much pain, I wouldn't be able to heal. It still hurt to be without Kelvin, and I was still trying to get over what could have been a great relationship. I was fully healed from my injuries, and Carlos pleaded guilty to kidnapping me and communicating threats. They took his mental state into consideration, so he was admitted into a hospital to get help. I was glad to have that all behind me.

I found myself a nice apartment, and I was enrolled in school. I was majoring in sociology. With a sociology degree, there would be plenty of jobs available helping people. That's what I wanted to do. I should have gone to counseling and allowed people to help me. The only downside is that some of the people on the campus recognize me as being "the accuser." After Mindy's interview, there was a newspaper article about me and my lifestyle, as they put it. My picture was attached to the article. The article was available online everywhere, and people would have access to those articles forever. Some people on campus would stare at me, and one girl who worked with the college newspaper asked if she could interview me, so people could see that I was in college now. I declined her offer. I thought it best that I remained silent and let people forget about me. Of course, with my name out there, I got calls from reporters, but I ignored all their calls. I was back in Little Rock and ready to start the next Chapter of my life. Latrice was glad I was back, and our relationship remained good. My parents came down hard on me after learning about what I had been doing for the last five years. It was hard for me to listen to it, but I knew they had every reason to be upset with me. I let them know how I felt about them abandoning me when Eugene and my affair became public.

My relationship with my parents was still strained but better. My mom had invited me over for dinner. She had cooked chicken pot pie, one of my favorite meals. I was looking forward to eating the pot pie, but I was still nervous about going because we hadn't spent any real time together since I've been back. Latrice and her family were going to be there, so it would be a nice buffer.

When I arrived, I helped my mother set the table. "I can't wait to sink my teeth into this pot pie," I said with a laugh.

My mom smiled. "Yes, I know how much you enjoy my chicken pot pie."

"Just make sure you save some for us," my father joked.

"I'll try."

Latrice and Steven, along with Casey, arrived shortly after me. I immediately took Casey out of her arms. "You are getting so big," I said to her as she smiled at me.

"She's crawling around getting into everything now," Steven said with a smile.

Steven was an attractive light-skinned man who wore glasses. After meeting me and getting to know me some, he decided that I wasn't so bad after all. We all sat at the table and began eating. We laughed as Casey made a mess of her food.

Everything was going well until my mom asked me a question. "So, have you spoken with Kelvin?" she asked.

Everyone became quiet, and I hated to be put on the spot

like that. I had told my mother about my relationship with Kelvin, now I wished I hadn't. I had been trying so hard not to think about him. "No, I haven't spoken with him."

"Why not?" she asked and then took a sip of her tea.

"Because right now, I'm focused on my studies and healing."

"I understand that, but a good man like him doesn't come around too often, and he's a doctor."

"I think it's good that Felicia is focused on school," Latrice said, coming to my defense. I smiled at her to let her know I appreciated that.

"I'm glad you're going to school, so you can make a good living and stop counting on making money the unethical way like you've been doing."

"Honey, let's not hassle Felicia," my father stepped in.

"I'm not hassling her; I'm just asking her questions. There is nothing wrong with that."

"Yes, I made a lot of money the unethical way as you put it, but that's all behind me now," I said.

"If it's all behind you now, then why haven't you stepped foot in a church since you been back in Little Rock? That would show that you are putting things behind you and healing."

"I'm not ready to go back to church yet."

"Excuses, excuses," my mother criticized, shaking her head.

"Jackie, please," my father said, desperately trying to get my mother to back off.

"That's okay, dad. I'm leaving now," I said and stood up.

"Don't leave, Felicia," Latrice pleaded with me to stay. Steven looked like a deer caught in headlights.

"So, you're still running away when things get tough," my mom continued.

"I appreciate the meal. Goodbye, everyone," I said, left the dining room and headed for the door.

I tried to have a better relationship with my mother, but it wasn't going to happen if she was going to keep judging everything I do or don't do. I couldn't win with her.

Chapter 20

Kelvin

These past months have been difficult. I missed Felicia, but I didn't want to be with a woman that everyone knew as "the accuser." I felt torn about walking away from Felicia the way that I had. She was hurt, vulnerable, and I'm sure she felt all alone, but I couldn't stay with her. My family was shocked after learning about the things Felicia did. Still, my mother felt like I should forgive her because she could tell I loved Felicia.

I did love her, but I had to get over her. I'm dating a beautiful woman named Amelia. She is light-skinned with glossy hair, and she is a nurse practitioner. She has a five-year old daughter named Skylar. She had been flirting with me and trying to get me to go out with her for the past year. She was happy to learn that I wasn't dating Felicia anymore, but she would ask me a lot of questions about her, wanting to know if I still had feelings for her. I told her no, of course. Her questions made me uncomfortable, and I can tell she was insecure when it came to Felicia. I went out with her as a distraction. She was getting serious about me, but I wasn't serious about her like that yet. She wanted to move way too fast. I think she was trying to desperately find a father for her daughter since her husband hasn't been to see her since they have been divorced. I wasn't serious about her yet, so I definitely didn't want to play father to her daughter. I had dinner with her and her daughter, and I felt uncomfortable because she was trying too hard to get me to bond with her daughter.

The plus side is that she was happy to accompany me to church. She was a Christian like me, but she kept trying to get me into bed. I was attracted to her, so it was hard to resist her, but I wasn't going to go there with her. That was reserved for the marriage bed. I also like her because she has a good career in the medical field like me. Felicia seemed to not have any real goals in life but to live off money she made by entrapping men.

I was to heading to Amelia's house because she was cooking dinner for me. When I arrived at her townhouse, I knocked on the door. Amelia answered with a huge smile on her face looking lovely in a pair of jeans and wine red shirt. She had her hair pulled back in a ponytail.

"I'm glad you made it come in," Amelia said and then stepped aside to let me enter.

My stomach growled at the nice aroma coming from the kitchen. "Dinner smells good," I complimented.

"Thanks, and it's done," she said, and I followed her into the kitchen.

Skylar was seated at the table. She was a pretty little girl, and she looked a lot like Amelia. "Hi, Mr. Kelvin."

"Hey there," I said.

Amelia cooked chicken pasta with ranch dressing, and we were having buttered rolls to go with it.

I helped Amelia with the plates, and then we joined Skylar at the table and began eating.

"This is delicious," I said to Amelia.

Amelia's face lit up. "I knew you would like it. It's nice of you to spend time with us like this."

"It's my pleasure. I try, but it's not easy with our schedules."

"Mr. Kelvin, can you take me to the park this weekend?" Skylar asked innocently.

I started to feel uncomfortable as Amelia and Skylar looked at me expectantly.

"I would really appreciate it if you would take her because I have to work this weekend," Amelia said, putting even more pressure on me.

This is what I didn't like. She was pressuring me to take Skylar to the park, just me and her, and I really wasn't comfortable with that. "I'm not sure if that's a good idea," I said.

"You don't want to take me?" Skylar asked with a sad look.

I didn't know what else to say. I didn't want to hurt Skylar's feelings.

Amelia was just about to say something else when my cell phone rang, and I was thankful for the distraction.

"Hey, son. Could you come by the house? It's something I really need to talk to you about?" my mother asked me. I could tell by the sound of her voice that something was wrong.

"What's wrong?"

"I really want you to come over and talk to you about this in person."

I was having a nice dinner with Amelia until I was put on the spot, so going to see her now wouldn't be a problem. "Okay, mom. I will be there."

"I'm sorry, but I have to go."

"Why?" Amelia asked with a frown on her face.

"Something is going on with my mom, so I have to go check on her."

"Oh my, but do you have to leave right now because I made a special dinner for you. I want to know why you're never interested in spending alone time with Skylar. Is it because you're still hung up on Felicia?"

I couldn't believe she was saying all this in front of her daughter. "I'm sorry, and I really appreciate you making dinner for me, but I have to go check on my mom. We can talk about this later," I said and stood up, letting her know that was the end of the discussion for me.

"Okay, I hope everything is okay with your mother. Maybe we'll be able to get together again soon.

"Hopefully, we will." I kissed Amelia on the check, said goodbye to Skylar, and left the house.

I was relieved to be out of that house. I drove out of her driveway, headed to my mother's house. I didn't want to come across as a jerk, but I felt more comfortable spending time with Skylar with Amelia present. She was just trying too hard to get me to bond with her. I know she told Skylar to ask me to take her to the park. She should let things happen naturally. My thoughts then went to my conversation with my mother, and I started to tense up. She had me worried. When I arrived at my parents' neighborhood, I drove on their block. My parents live in a nice spacious, brick three-story house. Once I was in front of their house, I quickly parked my car, ambled up the driveway, and knocked on the door.

My mother answered the door with a strained look on her face. She stepped aside to let me in and I hugged her.

"Now, please tell me what's wrong because the look on your face is scaring me."

"Let's go in the den to talk," she said and started walking towards the den.

I followed her to the den feeling confused about what was going on. We sat on the sofa. I anxiously looked at my mother, waiting for her to tell me what was wrong.

"It's your father. He's been experiencing back pain and has some difficulty walking. He almost fell walking down the church steps last Sunday. I think something is seriously wrong, but he refuses to go to the doctor."

"Where is dad now?" I asked, growing worried.

"He's still at work. I want you to talk to him. He's so stubborn, but you're a doctor. You specialize in this sort of thing, so he should listen to you."

"I hope so, I'm going to talk to him now. You hang in there, mom," I said and kissed her on the cheek.

I left the house and drove to my father's business. I had a good idea what was wrong, but for the first time, I hope I wasn't right.

Chapter 21

Kelvin

When I arrived at my father's job, I saw his SUV parked out front along with another vehicle. I parked my car next to his and went inside the building. Denton walked from the back. He was in his mid-thirties and had been working for my father for ten years.

"Hey, Kelvin. Your father is in his office. I'm glad you're here because he won't come out of there, and he snapped at me when I asked him was everything okay. I'm supposed to be off now, but I've been hanging around to see if he'll emerge from his office."

"I appreciate you staying over, but you can go home now. I've got it from here."

"Okay, tell your dad I'll see him tomorrow," he said, and left the building.

I walked to the back of the building where my father's office was located and knocked on the door.

"I said go away, Denton. You should be off the clock anyway!" my father yelled.

I was shocked at the amount of anger I heard in my father's voice. I wanted to surprise him, so I opened the door and walked in. My father was sitting behind his desk and looked shocked to see me. "Kelvin, what are you doing here?" he asked.

I scrunched up my nose at the foul aroma in the room. I walked over to his desk, stood in front of him, and was horrified to see that he had soiled his pants. My father looked embarrassed, and I wondered what he would have done if I hadn't shown up.

"Dad, it's okay. Let's get you cleaned up."

"How? I didn't bring any extra clothes with me."

"Don't worry about it. I'll go by the house and get them."

"No, don't do that. I don't want your mother to know."

"You can't keep this sort of thing from her."

"I know, but just bring me some of your clothes or something. I just don't want her to know about this now. I know she told you I've been having some problems. That's why you're here, right?"

"She thought I might be able to help. You have a son who is a doctor; you should take advantage of it. You're going to the hospital to get checked out first thing in the morning. I'm going to bring you some clothes," I said and began walking towards the door.

"Kelvin, what do you think it is?"

I was hoping I was wrong at first, but the condition I found him in let me know I was indeed right.

I turned around and looked at my dad. "I think it's a spinal tumor."

Chapter 22

Felicia

I just got home from school, and after making something to eat, I was going to get started on the paper that I had to write. I was glad school was occupying most of my time because it took my mind off the argument I had with my mother. My mother called and apologized and admitted that she came down too hard on me. I forgave her, but I wasn't going to have dinner there anytime soon. I sat my books down in the living room and then went to the kitchen to make myself a sandwich when there was a knock on my door.

I was surprised someone was at my door because I wasn't expecting any company. I went to the door and looked through the peephole and was stunned to see Eugene standing there. *What is he doing here?* I asked myself. I stood there for a moment as I contemplated what to do. When he knocked again, I decided to let him in. I guess I couldn't avoid him forever.

I opened the door. "You better have a good reason for being on my doorstep," I said in an aggravated tone.

"Well, it's nice to see you too. Can I come inside?"

I stood there staring at him, hating the fact that he was still so handsome. His church was aired on tv, but I never watched it. He was dressed nicely in a cream-colored shirt and black jeans. Eugene was tall and had a nice build, and his dark skin was blemish-free. He was now in his mid- forties, and the years had been kind to him.

I didn't say anything; I just stepped aside to let him enter my apartment. He walked inside, and I closed the door behind him, walking into my living room. Eugene looked around my apartment.

"This is a nice place you have," he paused and looked me over. "And you are looking gorgeous."

"How did you know where I lived?" I asked, ignoring his compliment. I didn't like him showing up at my apartment like this. I had enough of men sneaking up on me.

"I have my ways of finding out things I want to know," he said and smiled at me.

"Well, I don't like you just showing up at my apartment unannounced."

"I'm sorry about that, but I wanted to come by to check on you because of all the things you've been through recently."

"Oh really? If you were so concerned about me, why did it take you this long to check on me? I've been here for about four months now."

"I know, but since everything came out about you and us, my past indiscretions have been put back into the spotlight. And Nadine has been keeping a close eye on me since she knows you're back in town. I've been thinking of ways to approach you, and I feel now is the time to talk to you."

Hearing him talk about how his past indiscretions were now back in the spotlight made me angry. It was my name being dragged through the mud. "I want you to get out now!"

"Whoa, calm down, Felicia. We need to talk about everything."

I laughed bitterly. "You want to talk now? You came back to me one last time, had sex with me, and then ignored my phone calls. Then I moved away to only find out I was carrying your child. I aborted it because I knew you wouldn't want it or me. It's a decision that I later regretted, and it hurt me deeply. It was all that pain that turned me into "the accuser," as everyone is referring to me now." Angry tears started spilling down my face.

Eugene's mouth was opened wide in shock, and all he could do was stare at me for a few moments. "I wish you would have told me you were pregnant. I honestly don't know what I would have done about the situation, but I would never have suggested that you have an abortion."

Hearing him say all of this only made me cry harder. Knowing he would have offered me some type of support only made me regret my decision even more.

Eugene put his arms around me. "I'm so sorry you had to go through that alone," he whispered in my ear as he gently rubbed my back.

Being in his arms brought back the old feelings I had for him, and before I knew it, we were kissing and removing our clothes, making love right on the couch. Afterwards, I laid in his arms and felt at peace. We both drifted off the sleep.

When I woke up, I was overcome with a deep feeling of remorse. It felt so good being with Eugene in that way again, but I didn't want to be that person again. I untangled myself from his arms and began to put on my clothes.

Eugene woke up and looked at me. "Come and lay back down with me," he said.

"No, we can't do this anymore. You should leave right now; I'm sure Nadine is looking for you anyway."

Eugene sat up and began putting his clothes on. "So, you're going to go there, huh?"

"It's the truth. I don't want to sneak around with you anymore."

"I understand. I really didn't come over here for this. We both were overwhelmed with emotions, and I realize I still have feelings for you."

"It doesn't matter because we can't do this again."

Eugene stood up, walked towards me, and kissed me softly on the lips. "I know we can't. Take care of yourself, and I'm sorry again about everything you went through."

Eugene left my apartment, and I just stood there, staring at the door. I finally got the closure I needed. Now I had to truly become a better person, and that meant getting back into church.

Chapter 23

Felicia

The following weekend Latrice and I were meeting up to have lunch at Linguini Town. It was a popular Italian restaurant, and I couldn't wait to order their Lasagna. When I arrived, Latrice had already arrived and was seated in the back in a booth.

I went over to join her. "Hey, you're looking good, mommy," I complimented. And she did. I loved the lavender blouse she was wearing, and her face was made up nicely.

"Thank you, but I'm off mommy duty today. I loved my daughter, but today Steven has her so I can have some time to go out and relax."

"That's good."

"Good afternoon, ladies. What can I get you to drink?" the waitress asked.

"I'll have an ice tea," I told her.

"And I'll have one too," Latrice paused. "And bring an extra ice tea."

"Okay. I'll bring those right out," she said and left the table.

"Why did you order an extra ice tea?"

"Don't get mad, but…." Her voice trailed off, and she looked over my shoulder.

I turned around to see my mother walking towards the table. I turned around and frowned at Latrice. "You invited her here? What were you thinking?" I whispered harshly.

Before Latrice could open her mouth to respond, my mother slid in the booth next to her. "Hello, daughter of mine, who keeps ignoring my calls."

I was quiet as I watched my mother. Her face identical to mine. Looking at her was like looking at myself twenty-five years for now, and I had to admit that she aged nicely. I ignored her and looked at Latrice. "What is she doing here?"

"So, you're going to ignore your own mother?"

"Felicia, you and your mother need to talk. You have to fix this thing between you."

"The thing that you are referring to is her turning her back on her own daughter while she worshiped the man who shamed me and broke my heart."

"No, sweetie. You shamed yourself by becoming a pastor's mistress."

"You know what? I'm not doing this," I said and shot up from my seat.

"Here are your drinks," The waitress said slowly as she approached our table. She was looking at all of us curiously. I could tell she could feel the tension.

I sat down to diffuse the situation.

"Are you ready to order yet?" she asked politely.

We told her our orders and she left the table.

"See, now it isn't so hard to sit down and have lunch with me," my mother said.

"I guess it isn't."

"I don't mean to put you down about your past, but I just don't want you to make the same mistakes again. You have so much going for yourself. You're back in college. I want you to have everything you deserve."

"Thanks, mom," I said. I could see the sincerity in her eyes. "I'm a different person now, and I will be back in church soon." I felt a twinge of guilt as I thought about my encounter with Eugene. I was going to erase that from my memory.

"That's great," she said.

I then looked at Latrice, who had a huge smile on her face.

She was happy that her little setup worked. The waitress brought us our food about twenty minutes later, and we enjoyed a nice conversation until we were interrupted.

"I know you were with my husband recently."

I could feel the anxiety coming on as I looked up at Eugene's wife, Nadine. Nadine is in her early forties and has a smooth caramel complexion. She was dressed elegantly as usual in black dress pants and a white blouse. She wore her hair out with a part in the middle. Nadine was gorgeous, even with the scowl that was painted across her face. "What are you talking about?" I asked to save face.

"Don't play dumb with me. Early this week, Eugene came home smelling like perfume. I knew it had to be you. I confronted him about it, and he denied it. Until I saw the text message he sent you yesterday talking about the amazing time you had together."

My face flushed with embarrassment. There was nothing I could do I was caught. I was angry with Eugene for being so stupid to send me a text and not erase it. I got that text, and I responded, telling that we did have an amazing time, but we couldn't do it again. I looked at my mother and Latrice, who were looking at me with disappointment. My mother and I were finally at a better place, and now Nadine had to come in here and cough up my secrets. What was she doing here anyway?

"So, you don't have anything to say for yourself, Felicia, the accuser?" She mocked.

"Nadine, there is no reason to make a scene," Latrice came to my defense.

"Oh, I'm not making a scene. You are so not worth it. I just want you to know that I know that you haven't changed despite what you want people to believe. Eugene told me how sorry he was, and it's me that he love, but I'm not so sure anymore. I told that man to stay away from you, but he just wouldn't listen. But I will tell you this if I find out you two have met up again, you both will be sorry," she said with so much coldness in her voice and eyes.

"Wait a minute, don't threaten my daughter!" my mother

said loudly, causing more people to stare at us.

"Oh, it's not a threat. It's a promise. I will not be made a fool of again. You have been warned," she said and marched away from our table.

"Before you let me have it, I want you to know that Eugene showed up at my apartment out of the blue, we started talking, and one thing led to another," I rambled on as my mother and Latrice frowned at me.

"I really believed that you are a changed person. Have you not learned from everything you went through with Carlos? Things have a way of catching up to you. Nadine is serious, so stay away from Eugene. He's no good, and she should divorce him anyway," my mother said.

"I know, mom, and I have changed. I just make a mistake with him."

My mother shook her head. "You can't go through life talking about I just made a mistake all the time. You still will have to suffer the consequences." My mother stood up. "Enjoy the rest of your day." And she left the table, leaving me stunned.

"I can't believe she just walked out on me. Every time she finds out something about me, she leaves my side."

"Can you blame her? She's so disappointed in you and so am I. It's Eugene who broke your heart, who led you to become this person that almost got you killed by Carlos. Then you come back to town and sleep with him?" Latrice asked me like it was the most ludicrous thing she ever heard.

"Now, you're judging me too."

"I'm not judging you, but you have to do better."

"I know that it was a mistake, that's all. Eugene and I both agreed it will never happen again, so Nadine has nothing to worry about."

"I hope for your sake that you really mean what you're saying," Latrice said while giving me a pitiful look.

We finished our lunch in awkward silence, and I felt like I had taken three steps back.

Chapter 24

Kelvin

The next day my mother and I were at the hospital. We were both saddened to learn that my father did, in fact, have a spinal tumor. I looked over his x-ray along with the neurosurgeon. The tumor was large, and removable but not without risks.

We talked it over with my father, and he was scared about all the risks. The risk he was the most concerned about was paralysis, but he was already losing function anyway. My brother Randall was on his way to the hospital. We were sitting in the lobby while they prepped my father for surgery.

"Kelvin, all this has made me realize how precious life is and how you should never take things for granted. No one wants to be without the person they love," she said as she stared into my eyes.

"Where are you going with this?"

"You need to try to get Felicia back because you love her, and I know you don't feel the same about Amelia. You don't talk about her with the same amount of passion that you talk about Felicia."

She was right; I didn't feel the same way about Amelia as I did about Felicia, but I had to give it time. And at least with Amelia, I knew what I was getting. "Things with Felicia won't work out. Amelia's great, and I want to see this relationship through."

"Okay, but I don't think you'll be truly happy with her," my mom continued.

"Don't worry about me, mom. We should focus on dad right now, because even if the surgery is successful, he will probably have to go through physical therapy."

"You're right, but still think about what I said."

Randall walked through the hospital door, and I waved him over. Randall and I could almost pass for twins, except he was a couple of inches shorter than me. Randall joined us in the chairs. His face was filled with worry.

"Dad's tumor is operable, but not without risks. The neurosurgeon, Dr. Miles, who is operating on him, is one of the best. He's in very capable hands."

"Will he be able to walk after the surgery?" Randall asked.

"There is a chance that he might not, but let's not focus on that. We just want him to pull through," I said.

Dr. Miles came over to us a few minutes later. "We're about to take Mr. Harris to surgery now."

"Can we see him before you take him to surgery?" my mother asked.

"Sure, but just for a moment because we need to go ahead and start the surgery."

We followed him to Dad's room. Randall looked like he wanted to burst into tears when he saw my father laying back in the hospital bed. I squeezed his shoulder for support. It was hard for all of us to see my father in this condition when he was usually so strong. We walked over to him.

My mother took his hand. "I love you so much," she said as her eyes became watery. "Let's pray."

We all joined hands and said a prayer over my father. Hopefully, God would answer our prayers.

Chapter 25

Kelvin

A few days later, I was at Amelia's house spending time with her. My father's surgery was successful, but he had to go through intense physical therapy. It had been a trying few days, and I was glad to be able to relax with Amelia.

Her daughter was upstairs asleep, and we were watching a movie on her couch. We were almost to the end of the movie when her doorbell began to ring.

"I'll be right back." She left the room.

I continued to enjoy the movie while she answered the door until I heard arguing. I got up and went to the door to see what was going on. Amelia was arguing with a man in the foyer area.

"What's happening here?" I asked as I looked back and forth between them.

The man looked at me and frowned. "Who are you?"

"I'm Kelvin. Who are you, and why are you arguing with Amelia?" I turned my attention to Amelia, and she had an embarrassed look on her face.

"I'm William, her husband. It's really none of your business, but I'm here to see my daughter because she's been keeping her from me."

I was stunned. He referred to himself as her husband, but she said they were divorced. Maybe he just said husband to get under my skin.

"You have no right to show up to my house unannounced, so leave," Amelia said angrily.

"I'm not leaving until I see my daughter, and you have this man around my daughter who I don't even know!" he yelled.

"Lower your voice. Skyler is asleep, and I don't want you disturbing her."

"She's my daughter. I'm not disturbing her. You've been keeping her away from me and contesting the divorce because you're mad that I left you. Our marriage wasn't working anymore, so I wanted to move on. Now give me the divorce and let me see my daughter."

"No," Amelia said spitefully with her mouth balled up.

I was shocked, and I had never seen this side of her before. I knew she could be jealous and pushy, but not evil like she was being now. She said she was divorced and that her ex-husband didn't want to have anything to do with her or her daughter, but that was obviously false. I didn't know what to say, and this had nothing to do with me, so I was going to leave.

William marched upstairs, and Amelia followed behind him, telling him not to wake her daughter. It really surprised me when Amelia punched him in the back. He yelled out that her constantly hitting him and being combative was the reason why he couldn't be with her anymore.

It was a dramatic scene that I wanted nothing to do with, so I exited her house and drove home.

When I arrived at home, my phone started ringing, and I saw that it was Amelia.

"Look I can explain," Amelia said hurriedly.

"There is nothing to explain. You lied to me. You don't want to let your husband go, but you want to be in a relationship with me too."

Amelia was quiet for a moment and then said. "You're right. I have been less than honest."

"You have things you need to figure out, so we shouldn't see each other anymore."

"No, I want to still see you. I'm falling in love with you."

"This isn't going to work. I'm not going to be in a relation-ship with a married woman. Find closure with your situation. Goodbye," I said and hung up.

I sighed. All this made me think of Felicia. It showed me that anyone was capable of surprising you and keeping secrets. Amelia was not the person I thought she was. Felicia wasn't perfect, but I felt a spark with her that I didn't feel with Amelia. It was time that we talked.

Chapter 26

Felicia

After making that mistake with Eugene, I rejoined another church and rededicated my life to God. The pastor Victoria Young was excellent. She talked to me one on one about all the issues I was dealing with. I had found my church home and my healing was beginning.

I've been keeping busy with school and church. I thought about getting another job, but I was living comfortably. I didn't have to worry about working right now, and that was good because I had a ton of work to do at school at times. Some of the college boys were constantly hitting on me, but I didn't want to be in a relationship right now. I needed to focus on myself. I had talked to my mother, and I was back on better terms with her.

I was sitting at the kitchen table working on an English assignment when my cell phone rang. It was Kelvin. My stomach started fluttering. I had been trying so hard to stop thinking about him, but he still managed to find his way into my mind. I was curious to know what he wanted since he hadn't called me once since everything was revealed about me. I answered it.

"Hi, Felicia. How are you?" Kelvin asked in an unsure voice.

I could tell he was nervous. "I've been well. What about you?"

"I've been hanging in there. I know you're surprised to hear from me, but I wanted to get together so we can talk."

"Yes, I'm surprised you called, but I'm not sure it's possible for us to meet since I moved back to Little Rock."

"Wow, when did you move back to Little Rock?"

"After I healed from my accident."

"Okay. Well, I don't have a problem coming to see you. I'm off on Saturday, so I can fly to Little Rock to see you if that's all right with you."

I couldn't stop myself from smiling. "Yes, that will be fine."

"Okay, I will see you on Saturday," he said, and we ended the call.

I sat there staring into space after the phone call, not believing Kelvin called me. I really didn't think he wanted to have anything else to do with me, and I couldn't blame him. I started back working on my paper, feeling excited.

When Saturday finally came, I was happy, but I had to remain rational. I know we couldn't resume our relationship. Kelvin called me about 12:00 p.m. to let me know he was at the airport. I offered to pick him up, but he said he would just take a cab to my place. I texted him my address.

I was nervous as I waited for him to arrive. I made sure I was looking good in a red blouse and blue jeans. Kelvin knocked on my door fifteen minutes later.

Kelvin smiled at me, looking me up and down. "Hey, you're looking good."

"So are you," I said as I took in his appearance.

I let him enter, and we went into the living room to talk.

We sat next to each other on the couch. "What have you been up to?" Kelvin asked me.

"I've rededicated my life to God, and I'm in college now, majoring in sociology."

Kelvin's face lit up. "That's great. I'm happy you've turned your life around. I've been doing well. My father had a spinal tumor removed, but he's expected to be okay."

"I'm sorry to hear that, but at least he will be fine."

We sat there staring at each other for a moment until Kelvin finally spoke again. "I would like for us to try again. I'm sorry how

I treated you. It was a lot for me to deal with all at once. No one is perfect, and I love you."

My heart warmed at his words, and I could tell by the look in his eyes that he meant it. I loved him too, but I didn't know if being with him right now would be the best thing for me. "I love you too, Kelvin, but I'm finally healing from all the hurt from my past. I don't think being in a relationship right now is the best thing for me. Things are going well for me, and I don't want to change my life around for another man. I did that once and became a totally different person. I finally know who I am now." Kelvin's face fell. I felt bad for crushing him, but I had to do what was best for me.

"I guess I understand, but I feel it in my heart that you are the right woman for me, so I'm not giving up."

He leaned forward and kissed me. The kiss became so passionate that we both had to stop ourselves before things went further. I never felt that amount of passion from a kiss, and for a moment

I felt bad about turning him down, so I felt the least I could do is hang out with him some. He did fly here to see me. I drove him around Little Rock, so he could see the city. We went to the mall and then had dinner.

After we finished dinner, I drove Kelvin to the airport, and he purchased a ticket to Vegas. He kissed me on the cheek and then boarded the plane. I watched as the plane took off. It hurt to see him go, and I tried to convince myself that I was doing the right thing by letting him go.

Chapter 27

Felicia

The next day after church, I went to Latrice's house to have dinner with her and her family. Latrice made a great dinner, and we sat at the dining room table to eat. We had good conversation, and I watched how she and her husband interacted. He was so loving toward her, and that made me think about Kelvin. I wondered if we could have the same thing.

After dinner, Latrice put Casey down for a nap, and Steven went to the den to watch football. Latrice and I went into the kitchen to clean up. I help her load the dishwasher.

"So, what's wrong? I noticed you got a little quiet at dinner."

I hadn't told Latrice that I talked to Kelvin. I was still trying to sort everything out in my mind, but now was a good time to tell her what was going on.

"Kelvin flew here yesterday to see me."

Latrice snapped her head towards me. "What, and you didn't tell me?"

"I know, but I was just trying to figure out how I feel about everything."

"So, tell me what happened?" Latrice asked as I handed her the final dish, and she put it in the dishwasher, closing it.

We sat down at the kitchen table, and I told Latrice everything that happened with Kelvin yesterday.

"Are you sure that's what you really want?"

"Not really, but how can it work out when I live here, and he lives in Vegas."

"All that can be sorted out. I feel like you two belong together. Are you sure you're not still angry with him for leaving you?"

I had to admit that it felt slightly good to turn him down after he abandoned me the way he did, but that was the old Felicia that liked to repay hurt with hurt.

"Maybe I am, but I'll consider trying to work things out with him." As soon as I said that, I felt much better.

"That's right. Don't let that good man get away," Latrice said with a smile.

Chapter 28

Kelvin

A couple of months passed by since I went to see Felicia, and I'm trying to move on with my life the best way I can. I really thought that Felicia would want to be with me again, but I should've known it wouldn't be that easy to get her back. I have been busy with work, but Felicia is still on my mind a lot. My father is getting better and stronger, and I'm happy about that. My mother isn't so stressed when I see her now.

Amelia had been desperately trying to get back with me, and I kept telling her it wasn't going to happen. Now she's been giving me attitude every time she sees me at work, which makes things awkward.

I had just finished going over an x-ray with one of the doctors when I was paged, saying I had a visitor. I left the lab and headed for the elevators wondering who could be coming to visit me. I took the elevator down to the first floor, walked down the hall by the lobby, and saw Felicia waiting for me. My mouth dropped open in surprise. She looked stunning in a simple pair of dark blue jeans, a yellow top, and heels.

As I approached her, she smiled. "Hi there, I know you're surprised," she said.

"Yes, I am, but I love being surprised like this, and you look beautiful."

"Thanks, is there somewhere we can go and talk? I really

need to talk to you about something."

"Sure, let's go to the cafeteria," I said and began leading her to the cafeteria.

We were just about to the entrance when Amelia walked up. I cringed inside because she had a frown on her face, and I knew things would not go well.

"I can't believe you. You won't give me another chance, but you want to be with trash like this."

"How dare you call me trash?" Felicia said angrily and took a step toward Amelia.

I stepped in front of Amelia. "You are way out of line," I said, feeling my anger start to rise. Amelia's behavior was uncalled for. People around us begin looking at us.

"Now you're defending her. She's just using you, and then she is going to ruin your life. And when she does, you are going to want to be with me again, a classy woman," she said, putting emphasis on "a classy woman."

Felicia was about to say something else when I jumped in. "Stop behaving like a jealous teenager," I said. Then Felicia and I walked by her into the cafeteria.

We found a seat at the back of the cafeteria. "Sorry about that," I apologized.

Felicia shook her head. "She claims to be classy, but she makes a scene in the middle of the hospital. So, what's the story between you and her?"

I knew that question was coming. "Amelia and I were in a relationship for a few months, and I ended things with her."

"Why?" Felicia asked.

"Is that really important?"

"Yes, it is to me, because I wasn't even aware that you had been in a relationship while we were broken up."

"She was still married while we were in a relationship."

"Wow," Felicia said as she took in everything I said, then she gave me a serious look. "Are you sure things are over between you two? Judging by how upset she was, she still has feelings for you?"

"Well, it's hard for her to accept that things are over between us, but they are for me. I never felt about her the way I feel about you."

Felicia gave me a small smile. "That is usually something guys tell a woman to make them feel special, but I can tell you really mean it."

"I do. Now please tell me why you're here." I was anxious to know why she was here, and didn't want to waste any more time talking about Amelia.

"It took me a couple of months, but I realize that I want to be with you, whatever it takes. I'm willing to transfer to a college here in Vegas."

"I'm glad to hear you say that. I couldn't stop thinking about you."

Felicia laughed. "Good because I booked a hotel room for a week."

"I get off at six. How about I take you out to dinner to celebrate us being back together?"

"I would love that," Felicia accepted, making my heart skip a beat.

Chapter 29

Felicia

On the third day of my visit, Kelvin invited me to be his date to the Hospital Director's house. He was having a dinner for his colleagues and some of his family. I was nervous, because mostly doctors were going to be there. I didn't want to do anything to embarrass Kelvin when we had been having such a good time.

"Come right on in, Kelvin. I see you brought a gorgeous date," The hospital director complimented as he stepped aside to let us in.

I didn't bring anything dressy, so I went shopping and bought a simple black dress. It was a classy dress. Kelvin looked nice in his black slacks and black and gray shirt. I looked around, admiring his opulent house.

"Felicia, this is Mr. Gregory Martin, our hospital director."

"Nice to meet you," I said and extended my hand.

"Likewise, I'm glad you two joined us. Some of our guests are already seated in the dining room. Grace, can you show them to the dining room." He said to the middle age maid who was coming around the corner.

"Sure, right this way," she said.

We followed her through the huge house until we were finally in the dining room. My mouth dropped to the floor when I saw Amelia sitting at the table. Mr. Martin walked in a moment later. When she saw us walk in, she smirked at us. I had a feeling this wasn't going to go well. Kelvin and I greeted everyone, and we sat down at the table. The maid brought out a few more dishes, and we all began eating.

"So, Felicia, what is it that you do?" Amelia asked with a haughty tone.

I was going to keep my cool. I could see she was trying to rattle me, but I wasn't going to play her game. "I'm in college."

"Oh really? What's your major?"

"Sociology."

"Okay, that's interesting, but it's not much you can do with a sociology degree."

"Is that really necessary?" Kelvin came to my defense.

Everyone at the table got quiet and looked back and forth between us.

"I'm sure she will put her degree to good use," Mr. Martin added.

"Yes, I'm really looking forward to graduation," I said.

"I bet you are. I couldn't imagine going to college at your age. I'm glad I finished in my early twenties." Amelia continued.

"That's good for you, but it isn't hard at all."

"I think it's great that you went back to college. Better late than never," One of his colleagues chimed in.

Seeing she was outnumbered, Amelia shut her mouth, and we all finished our dinner. I enjoyed the conversations. I thought I would be bored listening to them talk about doctor talk, but they talked about everything, politics, movies, and some of the places they traveled. I excused myself and went to the bathroom.

Once in the bathroom, I relieved myself, washed my hands, and touched up my makeup. I was about to walk out the door when my cell phone rang. I pulled it out of my purse and saw it was Eugene calling. I had been ignoring his texts. We didn't have anything else to talk about as far as I was concerned.

I answered the call to see what he wanted, even though everything in me was telling me it was a bad idea. "What do you want, Eugene?"

"Well, hello to you too. Have you been reading my texts?"

"Yes, it's nice to know that you missed me and can't stop thinking about me after that day, but you have to put it out of your mind because Nadine threatened me. And you for that matter."

"Don't worry about that. She's not going to do anything."

"You say that because you didn't hear her say it and saw the look in her eyes."

"I know we can't do it anymore, but I just can't stop thinking about you. I thought I had put you out of my mind until you came back to Little Rock, and we had sex again. I need you and that in my life again," he said with a chuckle.

"The sex between us has always been amazing and the sex we had recently succeeded that, but we got caught up in the moment. Let the past stay in the past. Besides, I moved on. I have a man now that loves me and only me. And he knows everything I have done, and he still loves me."

"You sound sure," Eugene said in a defeated voice.

"I am. I can't go down that road with you anymore."

"I understand. Take care of yourself, and I will never forget about you."

"I don't think I can forget about you either," I said, meaning it. I ended the call and then took a moment to gather myself.

I opened the door and was startled to see Kelvin standing in front of the door. "So you recently slept with Eugene?" he asked with so much hurt on his face.

"It's not what you think?"

"Okay, what is it that I think? Because I think I heard you talking to your ex-lover about how good your recent sex was," he said angrily.

His words made me defensive. "You're the one sneaking up on me and have your ex-girlfriend sitting in the dining room having dinner with us while trying to belittle me."

A frustrated look came across Kelvin's face. "I didn't know she was going to be here. But that doesn't even matter. You're still full of secrets. I can't believe you hopped back in his bed after everything that happened."

"It didn't happen like that. And I didn't do anything wrong. We weren't together, and you're the one that went off and got a girlfriend," I shot back.

"Is there trouble in paradise?" Amelia asked with an amused look on her face as she walked towards us.

I wasn't in the mood for her games. "Shut your mouth, you passive-aggressive hussy."

Amelia clapped her hands. "And there it is. The real trashy you has now emerged. I wasn't buying the classy act that you were putting on."

"Amelia, stay out of this," Kelvin said in a sharp tone,

"Look, I came to use the bathroom. I didn't know you and your girlfriend would be arguing in front of the bathroom. Now tell me, Kelvin. How do you think this could possibly work? Once trash always trash," Amelia said snootily.

I was boiling inside at this point. "Kelvin, take me home now!" I said, marching down the hallway and out the door, ignoring the guests' confused looks.

I tried to open Kelvin's car door and the alarm went off. I put my hands over my ears as the alarm beeped loudly.

Kelvin hurried outside and quickly quieted the alarm. We got inside his car and he drove me back to my hotel. Kelvin didn't say a word the whole ride. He parked the car in the hotel parking lot.

I stared at him. I could see the angry look on his face. "So you're not going to say anything? You just me want to get out of the car?" I asked, surprised that he was being so cold, but then I thought about how he broke up with me in the hospital. Was he going to leave me again?

Kelvin stared straight ahead. "Felicia, get out of my car."

"Are you breaking up with me?" I asked as I felt tears burning the back of my eyes.

"I need to think; just go."

I stared at him a moment longer. I wanted him to turn and look at me or something. Once I realized he wasn't going to budge, I got out of the car, slammed the door and stomped away from the car. I was angry. He told me he loved me, and now he was going to walk away from me again because of my mishap with Eugene.

Chapter 30

Kelvin

"So, are you going to tell me what happened?" My mother asked me. She had just finished making sure my father was comfortable upstairs in their bedroom before joining me in the den.

After what happened at the dinner party, I decided to go to my parents' house to clear my mind. But my mother could tell right away that something was wrong. I stared blankly at the basketball game on TV.

"You're not watching that game, Kelvin, so you might as well tell me what's going on."

"It's Felicia. She went back to Little Rock and slept with the same Pastor that drug her name through the mud."

A thoughtful look came across my mother's face. "I see, so let me guess when you found out you walked away from her again?"

"Yes, but I told her I needed to think about everything."

"You two were over at the time, and you were dating Amelia."

I blew out a frustrated breath. "That's exactly what she said. But it's the fact that I thought she changed. Why would she hop back in bed with him?" I was so angry about that.

"Did you ask her why?"

"Yes, but we really didn't get into the reason."

"Don't let this get in the way of what you two have. She's not still seeing him, is she?"

"I don't think so, but I overheard her telling him what a great time that had together, but she did say that she was in a relationship and that they can't be together."

"Okay, so you have your answer. Let it go."

"I want to, but I just can't help to think there are more things that I'm going to find out about her that I might not be able to handle."

"Relationships are about discovering things about each other as you go along."

Everything my mother said was right. I couldn't shake the fact that Eugene still had a hold on her. I couldn't get it out of my head that she told him that she would never forget about him. "I guess I should go and talk to her," I said.

"Yes, you should."

I continued to watch the game and my mother nudged me. "What are you waiting for?"

"I'll talk to her tomorrow. She was very upset when she got out of my car."

"That's why you should go and talk to her. Don't give a chance to fester."

I kissed my mother on the cheek. "Thanks for the talk," I said and left.

I drove to the hotel Felicia was staying at and went up to her room. I knocked on her door, and she opened the door a few seconds later. I watched as the surprised look on her face turned to one of anger.

"What do you want, Kelvin?"

She's not going to make this easy for me, I thought. "We need to talk."

Felicia didn't say anything as she stepped aside to let me in the room. Once inside, she closed the door. She was wearing a light pink silk robe. She looked beautiful in it, and for a moment, my mind wandered to what she was wearing under it, if anything at all. I could smell the fresh scent of body wash on her.

Felicia sat down on the couch in the room, and I sat next to her. She was watching an earlier episode of Grey's Anatomy.

"Felicia, I shouldn't have ended our night the way that I did, but it upset me to hear you talking to Eugene on the phone, and you told him you will never forget about him."

"I know that hurt you, but I won't forget about him because he was an important part of my past. But there is nothing for you to worry about because the way I feel when I'm with you isn't anything like what Eugene and I had."

My heart leaped when she said that. "I love you very much, Felicia, and I don't want anything to get in the way of that. I don't want you to keep anything from me."

"I won't, but you can't walk away from me every time you find out something you don't like."

I raised my eyebrow. "Why you say that? You plan to keep surprising me with stuff every month?"

Felicia playfully slapped me on the thigh. "No, but it cuts me deeply when you turn your back on me like that. You tell me you love me, but you are quick to throw me away like a piece of trash."

"You are not a piece of trash to me," I said and leaned forward, kissing her. She kissed me back and the kiss heated up. I opened her robe and ran my hands over her body.

"Let's stop," Felicia said as she panted.

"I don't want to. I want you right now." I had to have her at that moment. I wanted to wait until we were married, but that went out the window for me.

Felicia didn't protest further. I pulled off her bra and panties and then undressed myself. I took a moment to admire her body. Her skin was beautiful and so soft. Felicia broke me out of my trance by pulling me down and kissing me deeply.

After we finished, I held her tightly, completely satisfied. "You know I'm not letting you go after this, right?"

Felicia giggled. "You better not."

Chapter 31

Felicia

A month went by, and things had been going well with me and Kelvin. So well that he proposed to me with a three-carat diamond ring. Of course, I accepted, and I couldn't believe that I was going to actually be a bride. I had been through so much, and now I was going to have a wonderful life with the man that I loved.

Latrice and my mother helped me plan my wedding. The big day was a week away, and I was slightly nervous. I just got this nagging feeling that something was going to go wrong. I felt like it was too good to be true. I shut those feelings aside, but it kept coming.

I got through the week at The University of Nevada. I really liked the college, and managed to make a couple of friends on campus, Rena and April. I usually shied away from friendships because it was hard for me to trust anyone, except my cousin. I liked them enough to ask them to be bridesmaids in my wedding. I had also developed a good relationship with Kelvin's mother. She really liked me, and I was a little shocked by that because most mothers would be leery of their son falling in love and marrying a woman with a background such as mine. But she was very forgiving, and I could tell she was a true Christian. My mother and my relationship had improved a great deal, but I still feel as if she hadn't truly forgiven me for the things I did in the past. I felt like my father had truly forgiven me, and he really liked Kelvin; my mother did too.

I arrived home from school that afternoon, nervous. My wedding day was tomorrow, and my family was flying in tomorrow. I talked to Kelvin, and he was anxious to marry me tomorrow. I then called Latrice. She was going to be my maid of honor.

"Hey, Felicia. Are you excited about tomorrow?"

"Yes," I said in an unsure voice.

"Wait a minute, what's wrong?"

"Latrice, I just can't shake the feeling that something is going to go wrong."

"Stop that; nothing is going to go wrong. It's just the devil trying to make you believe that you don't deserve to be happy."

I considered what she was saying. She was right. A part of me still felt like I didn't deserve to be happy, but I really did feel like something was off. I couldn't explain it. I just did.

"Maybe you're right," I said, so Latrice wouldn't worry.

"I know I'm right. Sorry, I couldn't be there with you tonight to ease your fears, but I couldn't get off work today."

"Yes, I know. You don't have to explain."

"Okay, I'll see you tomorrow, and don't let those negative thoughts get the best of you."

"I won't." We ended the call.

I fixed myself something to eat, and then I watched TV for a little while before going to bed. It took me a while, but I finally fell asleep. I awakened when my bedroom door slowly creaked open. I turned around and was frozen in fear when I saw someone walk over to me, holding an object. And before I could scream, I was struck over the head.

I came to when I felt water being splashed into my face, and was scared out of my mind to see Carlos standing over me with a menacing look on his face. His appearance was rough, like he hadn't slept in days. I noticed I was inside some type of abandoned building and was tied down to a chair. There was a strong odor in the room. *What is going on?* I asked myself and then remembered someone coming into my room and hitting me over the head. I tried to move, but it was no use because the ropes were tied tight. I started to scream, and Carlos laughed.

"No one will hear you; it's the middle of the night. If you scream again, I'm going to duck-tape your mouth."

"How did you find me, and why do you keep following me? And how did you manage to get me out of my apartment?" I was planning to sell the condo I had bought. I was renting a townhouse, and I didn't think Carlos knew anything about it. I was tired of all this. I hadn't heard from Carlos in all this time, and now he pops up again on my wedding day.

"It's easy to find you. I have certain connections like I keep telling you. I just took you out the front door. You live in a quiet neighborhood, and no one was outside at the time. And I know you're getting married tomorrow. It's on your social media account. You don't deserve to be happy after what you did to me."

"I'm sorry about what I did to you, but I'm a different person now. You should just focus on your wife and try to get better."

That must have made him angry because he stepped closer to me and slapped me in my face. My head snapped back and my face stung from where he slapped me, and as he backed away from me, he held his back and winced in pain.

"So now you want me to focus on my wife since you've supposedly turned your life around, but I don't care if you have changed. Because of you, I'm probably going to have back pain for the rest of my life. You won't get your happily ever after. Today will be the day that you die. No wedding for you," he said and then put a piece of tape over my mouth, walking away.

I watched as he walked towards the door of the building. I was confused about what he was going to do until he got to the exit. He took a lighter out of his pocket, flicked it, and threw it on the floor. I watched in horror as the fire spread around each corner of the room. Carlos walked out of the building, and then a fire started outside the building. *Oh my God, he's going to burn me alive.* I realized, and tears started leaking from my eyes.

I couldn't believe I had come this far and was so close to a fairytale ending only to be burned alive.

Chapter 32

Kelvin

I was nervous and scared as I paced back and forth in one of the rooms to get word that Felicia had arrived. The wedding was supposed to start two hours ago, and she was a no show. I had called her repeatedly, but my calls went unanswered.

"Sit down and try to calm down. She will be here. I'm sure she has a perfectly good explanation for being late," Randall said, trying to encourage me.

I stopped pacing and sat down. "I don't know. Felicia has a lot of issues. I thought she got over it for the most part, but maybe I was wrong."

"Stay here. I'm going to talk to her family to see if they know something," Randall said and exited the room.

As I sat there waiting for Felicia to arrive, I started thinking about Gabrielle and how she humiliated me on what was supposed to be my last wedding day. No, this couldn't be happening again. To be humiliated a second time would just be too much for me, and I could feel myself breaking down.

There was a knock on the door. "Come in," I said.

In walked Latrice and Felicia's mother, Jackie. "I'm sure Felicia has a good reason for not being here yet. She was a little worried last night about something going wrong, but I tried to convince her that she was wrong," Latrice said.

"My daughter has been known to run away, but I can tell by

how she talks about you that she loves you. She was really looking forward to marrying you, so I don't know where she could be right now," Jackie said.

"We went by her condo, and her car was there. I knocked on the door and she didn't answer. Maybe she went for a walk for something," Latrice said, but I could tell she didn't believe what she was saying because she had a worried look on her face.

I was just about to respond when my mother opened the door. "Kelvin, the police are here. It may have something to do with Felicia," she said frantically.

Hearing that, I sprinted out of the room with Latrice and Jackie right behind me. When I got to the front of the church, two police officers were standing there with grim looks on their faces, and my heart dropped. The guests were standing around, looking curious.

"Are you Kelvin Harris?" one of the officers asked.

"Yes, I am."

"Did something happen to my daughter?" Jackie asked anxiously, and Felicia's dad stepped behind her, putting his hand on her shoulder.

"Felicia Murray was found in an abandoned burning building by firefighters. They were able to get her out in time, but she's unconscious from smoke inhalation. I'm not sure about the severity of her injuries.

"Oh my God!" Latrice hollered out.

"What hospital is she at?" I asked, anxious to get to her.

"Wait, there's more. We pulled Carlos Dutton over because he was driving at a high rate of speed. When we pulled him over, he smelled like gasoline and we found two gasoline containers in his back seat. So we figured that he took Felicia to an abandoned building and set the building on fire with her tied up inside," the officer paused for a moment before he continued. I knew what he was about to tell us was going to be bad. "When the officers went to arrest Carlos, he pulled out a gun from his pocket and was about to shoot, so the officers opened fired on him. He was killed."

At that moment, I felt no remorse for Carlos. I was concerned about Felicia, and how scared she would have been thinking she was about to die again. I couldn't believe Carlos had popped back up. I thought he was still in the hospital getting help. I should have researched him to see what was going on with him. I should have been there to protect Felicia, and I felt even more guilty for doubting her.

Chapter 33

Felicia

I slowly opened my eyes, and the first face I saw was Kelvin. I tried to say something but couldn't because a tube was down my throat, and I began choking. Kelvin darted out of the room and came back with the doctor and a nurse.

The nurse gently removed the tube from my throat, and I began coughing. "Miss Murray, do you know what happened to you?" the doctor asked me.

"Yes," I said hoarsely. I remembered everything, and I was happy to know that I was alive.

"Miss Murray, you inhaled a lot of smoke, but it is a good sign that you remember what happened. I'm going to check your vitals. Right now, I'm concerned about your lungs and heart," the doctor said. "Everything looks good, but you will have to stay the night for observation," he said and then left the room along with the nurse.

Kelvin took my hand. "Baby, you gave us all quite a scare. I'm sorry I didn't protect you. We should have been more cautious about Carlos. There is something else you should know. Carlos was killed by the police when then they tried to arrest him. He pulled out a gun and was about to shoot them."

I was overcome with so much remorse. As I looked at Kelvin and saw so much love and concern in his eyes, I didn't think I deserved him. "You deserve someone better than me. I don't think we should get married because I will ruin your life. Even though Carlos is gone, there may be other men from my past that may want to get back at me."

"Don't think like that. I want to be with you. You deserve to be happy. I know you feel guilty about what happened to Carlos, but he should have gotten help. It's unfortunate that Carlos had to die, but at least he can't hurt you anymore."

"But what about the other men from my past? Or maybe Mindy?" I asked as my mind went crazy with all the possibilities.

"Don't drive yourself crazy about things that probably aren't going to happen. You suffered a lot, and Carlos almost killed you twice. Don't let him or the things you did in the past weigh you down."

His words brought me comfort. He was right. I had survived, so now it was time to go get my happiness. "You're right, and I love you," I whispered.

"I love you too," Kelvin said and kissed me on the lips. "I'm going to send in your family because they're worried about you."

"Bring them in," I said.

Kelvin left the room, and my parents and Latrice came into my room with heartbroken looks on their faces. But Kelvin's words had encouraged me, and I told them not to worry because I was going to be all right, and for the first time in a while, I truly believed that.

Chapter 34

Felicia

A month later, Kelvin and I were standing at the altar looking into each other's eyes. I could feel the love pouring from Kelvin's eyes. We waited a month to give myself time to heal physically and mentally. The media started to talk again when what Carlos did to me got out. People showed me sympathy, but they were also sad that Carlos was killed in the manner he was. He had a mental illness, and people were sympathetic about that. Mindy trashed me in the media and started the rumblings again about me being "the accuser," but I didn't let it get to me this time. I prayed and went to church, and I knew I was forgiven for my past sins. And my heart was on the way to being fully healed.

As we looked into each other's eyes as the minister pronounced us husband and wife while our family and friends looked on, I knew Kelvin and I were going to be happy together. I could feel it in my spirit.

When we were pronounced husband and wife, Kelvin and I shared a passionate kiss. I finally felt completely healed through the love and grace of God. I didn't have the weight of being "the accuser" on my shoulders anymore.

Take A Look At What's Coming Next:

www.majorkeypublishing.com/sneakpeeks

COMING NEXT!

CHECK OUT THESE SNEAK PEEKS!

WWW.MAJORKEYPUBLISHING.COM/SNEAKPEEKS

Be Sure To Check Out Our Other Releases:

www.majorkeypublishing.com/novels

To submit a manuscript to be considered, email us at submissions@majorkeypublishing.com

Be sure to LIKE our Major Key Publishing
page on Facebook!